S~~a~~
The ~~~~
Witch®

"We've got a major problem! And I mean major!"

"What? What is it?" Hilda asked as she rushed in from the kitchen.

"What's wrong?" Zelda asked as she hurried into the room.

"I cast a spell," Sabrina said, heading over to the couch but feeling too tense to sit. "And now all my friends have magic and I've lost my powers."

There was an incredibly long silence while her aunts looked at each other. Sabrina braced herself for the lecture of her lifetime.

"Sabrina, you should sit down," Zelda said in a soothing voice. "We thought you had gotten over this years ago."

"Gotten over what?" Sabrina asked as she reluctantly sat down.

"Losing your powers," Hilda added, then prodded her niece's memory. "When you turned sixteen."

"What are you talking about?" Sabrina asked as she got that sinking feeling in her stomach. This was definitely not the kind of talking-to she had expected.

Titles in Sabrina, the Teenage Witch® Pocket Books series:

Topsy-Turvy

Paul Ruditis

Based upon the characters in Archie Comics

And based upon the television series
Sabrina, The Teenage Witch
Created for television by Nell Scovell
Developed for television by Jonathan Schmock

POCKET
BOOKS

LONDON • SYDNEY • NEW YORK • TOKYO • SINGAPORE • TORONTO

POCKET
BOOKS

First published in Great Britain 2002 by Pocket Books
An imprint of Simon & Schuster UK Ltd
Africa House, 64-78 Kingsway
London WC2B 6AH

First published in 2002 by Simon Pulse,
an imprint of Simon & Schuster Children's Publishing
Division, New York

POCKET BOOKS and colophon are registered
trademarks of Simon & Schuster
A CIP catalogue record for this book is
available from the British Library

ISBN 0 7434 4109 5

1 3 5 7 9 10 8 6 4 2

For Sarah, Emma,
and Moira

Chapter 1

☆

"**H**as anyone seen Josh?" Sabrina asked for the tenth time since entering the bull pen of the *Boston Citizen*.

And for the tenth time, she received the same response: "No."

Sabrina had been all over the office looking for him since reporting for work that afternoon. Obviously he must have been out covering a story. Josh was the best photographer Sabrina had ever met. Since he'd graduated from college last year he had managed to land a job as photographer for the *Citizen*, one of the city's premier newspapers. Josh was also instrumental in having Sabrina hired as an intern.

"Sabrina, did you distribute that memo to the staff yet?" Mike, the paper's editor, interrupted her search for Josh.

"Memo?" Sabrina was momentarily clueless as to what he was talking about, but she recovered smoothly. "Oh, the memo! Right. The copier was out of ink. I was just getting more to refill it."

"Good job, Spellman," he said. "Way to stay on top of things."

"By the way," she continued as she looked on her desk for the missing memo. "Is Josh out on a story?"

"Yep. But he should be back soon," Mike said as he returned to his office.

Sabrina found the missing document as soon as her boss walked away. She hadn't actually lied about the copier being out of ink. She had tried to use it earlier to copy some of her school-work. However between then and now, she had spent all of her time looking for Josh to tell him some exciting news.

Sabrina grabbed the memo and stopped by the storage closet to pick up a bottle of ink before heading to the copier upstairs. Normally she would have used the one in the bull pen, but a repair guy was currently working on that copier for the third time this month. As soon as Sabrina reached the top of the stairs, Josh walked into the downstairs part of the office, settled into his desk, and reloaded the film in his camera without ever seeing Sabrina.

Sabrina went to work on refilling the ink in the copier. The last two times she had done this particular task she'd spilled ink all down her front, so she looked around to make sure no one was coming and gave a little point of her finger to let magic help with the job. With the ink in the machine, Sabrina set to the task of copying. She knew she could have made copies of the memo using her powers as well, but her aunts had always taught her not to abuse her witchly gifts since it would be unfair to mortals if she used her natural advantages to get her work done. From time to time, Sabrina and her aunts had relied on magic to help them out of certain situations, but overall they'd tried to live as mortals in the Mortal Realm.

As the machine pulled the two-page memo through its inner workings, Sabrina finally had time to stop and reflect on the great day she was having. First she had gotten an A on her astronomy paper. This wasn't a major accomplishment; Sabrina had always gotten good grades in both high school and college. The big news was that her astronomy professor had submitted her paper to be considered for publication in the school's annual science journal, the *Adams Researcher,* which consisted of some of the student body's best work. And Sabrina wasn't even a student in the science department.

It was rare for a non-major to even be considered, and even more uncommon to actually be included. Sabrina was totally shocked when her professor informed her that she was going to be only the fifth non-science major in Adams's history to have a paper accepted in the *Researcher*.

The day kept getting better, as she learned of good grades in her classes. That was until she was called to the office of the college president that afternoon. But Sabrina wasn't nervous. This wasn't the first time she had spoken with President Banning since he'd been dating her Aunt Hilda on a fairly regular basis. In the meeting she was thrilled to learn that she was nominated and chosen to receive the school's annual alumni scholarship. After President Banning had gotten through convincing Sabrina that an impartial panel chose the students—as opposed to him choosing his girlfriend's niece—Sabrina was properly overjoyed. The scholarship wouldn't pay for her remaining years at Adams, but it would certainly help with her current semester's tuition.

After leaving the president's office, Sabrina had to go directly to work at the *Citizen*, so she didn't have the chance to tell any of her friends or family about her great news. She had hoped to see Josh when she got to work, figuring that she could at least share her news with him, but he was out on assignment. Sabrina was going crazy and about to burst if she didn't tell someone, and that's about when the copier decided to burst as well, getting a paper jam.

After fixing the paper jam, it wound up taking Sabrina over fifteen minutes to finish making copies for the staff. Add to that the time it took to distribute the memo to the upstairs offices and it was quite a while before Sabrina got back to the bull pen, where she found Josh's desk was once again vacant. Sabrina finished dropping off copies of Mike's memo before stopping by his office. "Hasn't Josh come back yet?" she asked as she handed the editor his original memo.

"Back and gone again," Mike said. "There was a small fire at the Bull and Finch Pub and I wanted him to get some photos of the place since it's a Boston landmark."

"Oh," Sabrina said as she slumped into one of his guest chairs.

"You seem more eager than usual to see Josh today," Mike noted. "Is something wrong? And remember, I don't really care to hear too much about the trials and tribulations of college life."

"No, nothing's wrong at all." Sabrina perked up at finally having someone to talk to. "I've just had the best day and I wanted to tell him all about all my good news. See, it started out—"

Just then, Mike's phone rang. "Yes," he said by way of answering the call, hardly waiting for Sabrina to stop speaking. "Actually, she's right here."

Sabrina had hoped it was Josh on the other end of the call, but she really couldn't imagine him calling up Mike to look for her.

"Oh, I didn't know you wanted to start right now," he continued into the phone. "I'll send her right over."

Mike hung up the phone and looked at Sabrina with a strange smile on his face. She had never gotten such a look from him and, quite frankly, it worried her. "Was that about me?" she asked, dying to know the cause of his expression.

"Yes, it was," he replied. "And I have some more good news that I think is going to make your day even better."

"I like the sound of that," Sabrina said even though she would have preferred to tell her story first.

"You've been living in Boston for a while now, right?" he asked.

"Well, since college," Sabrina said. "But before that I was just over in Westbridge, which is pretty much the same as being in Boston."

"But you do know about the Freedom Trail?" Mike asked.

"Of course," she said, and then began to recite what she remembered from a report she had done on the subject while she was in high school. "It's one of America's first historic walking tours serving as the perfect introduction to Colonial Revolutionary Boston. A red brick or painted line connects various historical sites on the trail and guides visitors through the several-hour walking tour covering two and a half centuries of the city's past."

"What did you swallow, a tour book?" Mike asked in his usual straightforward manner.

"Just trying to be thorough," Sabrina replied as she shifted uncomfortably in her chair. Mike was a pretty nice guy, but every now and then he had a tendency to be a bit of what her aunt Zelda would call a "curmudgeon." However Sabrina always found that aspect of him to be part of his charm as a newspaper editor.

"That's what I like about you, Spellman," Mike said, giving her a warm smile. "And that's why I'm putting you on a new assignment that's a little bigger than those college columns you've been doing for me."

Sabrina totally perked up at this bit of news as she magically conjured up a notepad and pencil and brought them out from behind her back so she could take notes on her latest assignment. Since starting her internship at the paper, she had done several small pieces geared to students her own age, but she had yet to do any reporting on subjects beyond college-level interest. "What's the story?" she asked, pencil at the ready.

"Spellman, you continue to amaze me," Mike said, regarding the sudden appearance of her writing utensils. "Have you had a chance to work much with Christy Caldwell since she came onboard?"

Sabrina shook her head "no," immediately dreading what the assignment could be. Christy had started working at the *Citizen* only a few weeks ago and quickly had a reputation for being somewhat intense. She had already sent one of the newer interns home crying, and he was a football player.

"Since Christy is new in town," Mike continued, "I'm having her write a special supplement on Boston tourism, focusing on the Freedom Trail as the main historic attraction."

"I like it," Sabrina said quite honestly—and not just for brownnosing points—although she knew that a positive attitude always helped when talking to the boss.

"I was hoping you would," Mike replied, with just a touch of good-natured sarcasm. "Anyway, since Christy isn't quite familiar with Boston yet, I thought it best to team her with someone who's lived here a while. And that person is you, Spellman."

"You want me to cowrite a special supplement?" Sabrina asked, shocked at being given such an awesome responsibility. "A shared by-line?"

Sabrina could already see her name in print on the supplement: *A Tour of Boston, by Christy Caldwell & Sabrina Spellman.* Although she would have preferred it to read: *Sabrina Spellman & Christy Caldwell.*

"Whoa there, kiddo," Mike said with a warm smile on his face. "We can't go giving interns that much credit. It makes the paid staff a little tense. I was thinking something more like, 'Written by Christy Caldwell' and then underneath that we'd add, '*with* Sabrina Spellman.' Of course, the print would be a bit smaller for your name."

"Sounds good to me." Sabrina wasn't one to quibble over silly little words and name placement, like most of the staff did. She was just happy that he trusted her with the job, knowing how rare it was for an intern to be given the chances she'd had to write for the paper.

Instead of worrying over the name placement, Sabrina was considering all the different ways she could approach the supplement. Naturally Christy would be the one in charge, since she was the paid reporter, but Sabrina knew it would be best to have ideas at the ready. Christy had been hard enough to please when Sabrina had tried to get the woman's ever-changing lunch order correct, so she couldn't imagine the reporter would be any less precise when it came to articles bearing her name.

Not just an article, Sabrina thought. *It's a supplement.*

Sabrina's mind was already picturing the little magazine insert for the newspaper, from the articles she wanted to write to the layout and design. She knew that reporters really had no say over layout and design, but since she was dreaming, she figured that she might as well dream big.

Sabrina also wished that Josh had been around so that he could come along and take pictures for the piece. Even though they worked in the same office, they had never really worked on anything together, unless she counted the times they had made cappuccinos together at the coffeehouse. But this was entirely different. Now she had even more exciting news to tell him. This was easily becoming one of the best days of her life.

"Christy is over at Boston Common," Mike roused Sabrina from her wandering thoughts, referring to one of the oldest public parks in the country and the location of the start of the

Freedom Trail. "She's waiting over there for you to meet her."

"Does she want me to bring any information on the trail?" Sabrina asked eagerly.

"No, just yourself," he replied. "She's got everything you need with her already."

"Thanks, Mike," Sabrina said.

"Don't bother thanking me," he replied. "Just get over to the Common."

"Will do," she said as she bounded out of her seat. "I'll make you proud."

"I'd settle for you making the deadline," Mike replied.

Chapter 2

"**S**ure, I can just head over to Boston Common and meet Christy," Sabrina said to herself as she continued to circle the park. "Far be it from her to tell Mike *where* in the park I should meet her."

Boston Common was a huge public park about fifty acres in size. Sabrina had begun looking for Christy at the State House, since that was the formal start of the Freedom Trail, but the reporter was nowhere to be found. From there she headed over to Charles Street, figuring she could circle the park once before actually going through its twisting walking paths. All the while she was hoping that Christy had not gone across the street to the Public Garden, since Sabrina knew she didn't have the time to look everywhere for the reporter.

At least Sabrina was lucky enough to have to search through the park on a nice warm day. Between school, the newspaper, and her job at the coffeehouse, she rarely had any time to get out to the park, so she figured she might as well enjoy the walk. The only thing keeping it from being pleasant was the fact that she knew that Christy was waiting for her, and considering the woman's personality, Sabrina imagined that the reporter was getting more and more annoyed with each passing minute.

Sabrina continued her search by the frog pond, but Christy was nowhere to be found. Plunging headlong onto the Common, Sabrina pushed her way though the trees and saw a familiar blond woman sitting at the foot of a statue. Unfortunately Christy had dark hair. The woman Sabrina had found was her aunt Hilda.

"What are you doing here?" Sabrina asked as she noticed a bouquet of flowers on the ground beside her aunt.

Hilda nearly jumped out of her skin, not expecting to hear a voice so close to her, much less one belonging to her niece. Meanwhile Sabrina felt a little charge out of the fact that she finally had someone she could share her good news with. She was near the bursting point.

"Don't tell Zelda you saw me here," Hilda implored before Sabrina could get another word out. The look on her aunt's face kind of suggested that this was not exactly a happy trip to the park.

Sabrina noticed the plaque on the statue read PAUL REVERE. Oddly enough, it was sitting in the center of a small grove of trees well off the beaten path. It was not exactly great placement for a statue honoring one of the legendary heroes of the Revolutionary War.

"I won't say a thing," Sabrina said as she bent to sit beside her aunt on the soft green grass, "as long as you tell me why I can't."

"Oh, it's just another one of those stories where Zelda thinks she's always right and I'm always wrong," Hilda replied.

Though she was tempted to make a joke, Sabrina knew that her aunt's tone implied she was not in a humorous mood. This was odd for Hilda, since she was always the fun aunt, while Zelda tended to be the responsible one.

"It happened over two hundred years ago," Hilda began her tale. "I used to date the man who became this statue."

"You went out with Paul Revere?" Sabrina asked, always surprised to hear about both of her aunts' numerous brushes with history. From Sigmund Freud to the wizard Merlin, both of her aunts had very interesting stories about the famous men they had dated. This is just one of the many benefits of being a witch and living for hundreds of years.

"I wish," Hilda retorted. "Paul Revere was at

least going someplace—usually on horseback at a high speed. No, I fell in love with a wayward minuteman named Richard Locksley."

"But the statue is of Paul Revere," Sabrina said, double-checking the plaque to make sure she was correct.

"That's just what the plaque says," Hilda replied. "It actually looks nothing like Paul, but after a few centuries, no one really notices."

"So this is a statue of Richard Locksley?" Sabrina asked.

"No," Hilda corrected her niece. "The statue *is* Richard Locksley. Or, he was at least, before Mother got a hold of him."

Sabrina knew that once her grandmother was involved, this had the makings of a good story, so she chose to remain silent as her aunt went on with the tale.

"You see, we had fallen in love around the start of the war," Hilda said with a wistful look in her eyes. "I was blinded by my feelings for him and thought he was a great hero, when, truth be told, he was really a deserter."

Suddenly, the world went all wavy and cloudy, and Sabrina could actually begin to see the events as her aunt described them. This was both one of the best and most annoying things about being a witch. It wasn't often that they could tell a story without getting an immediate instant replay in the form of a flashback. At times it got to be a bother having the world get all wavy and distorted, but being able to see the events as they unfolded generally made story-telling easier, as it really cut down on the work involved in setting the scene.

"It was the late seventeen hundreds," Hilda continued as she and her niece focused on the action playing out before them. "And I was just over four hundred years old."

In the flashback Sabrina saw her aunt dressed in Revolutionary garb, sweeping up a partially wooden and partially dirt floor. She silently made a note of thanks for being born when she was. The outfits Sabrina wore every day were much more comfortable than those big, bulky dresses. And that's to say nothing of houses with electricity and indoor plumbing.

Her aunt looked only slightly younger than she did now. Whenever Sabrina saw either of her aunts in flashbacks—or old pictures, and even in paintings—she was always amazed at the fact that she was looking at them hundreds of years ago. She also got a little excited by the idea that hundreds of years from now she too would con-tinue to look young.

"Richard was a mere twenty years old," Hilda went on. "I had been in love with mortals before, but he was the first one who had ever made me forget about Drell. And considering we're talking about a mortal as opposed to the all-powerful head of the Witches' Council, that was quite a feat for Richard back then."

Sabrina had almost forgotten about her aunt's involvement with Drell, because it had been so long since she had seen the two of them together. Hilda was much happier dating President Banning.

Hilda let the story play out before them as Sabrina watched the flashback.

"You should not be here," eighteenth-century Hilda said to her love. "My sister will be back soon."

"I could not stay away," Richard replied as he pulled her into his arms. "The war rages on, but I cannot go back into battle without at least one kiss."

"This is better than one of those romantic historical movies," Sabrina said as she watched the scene. She was almost tempted to zap in some popcorn.

"You should not be here with me unescorted," Hilda of the past continued as she pushed him away. "What will people think?"

"I think you have more pressing concerns of propriety," Richard said rather cryptically.

Just then both Sabrina and the pair she was watching heard a noise coming from the front of the house. Someone was walking up the path to the door. Suddenly the action in the flashback grew more frantic as Hilda hurried her beau out of the room.

"'Tis my sister," Hilda said as she pushed Richard into the next room. "You must hide. I'm afraid of what could happen if she saw you."

"A kiss, first," Richard begged as Hilda started to shut the door. Pausing for a moment, she granted his request.

"Now remain silent." She shut the door to the room as the front door to the house opened and an over-two-hundred-years-younger Zelda came in.

"Where is he?" Zelda asked as soon as she crossed the threshold.

"Where is who? Or whom? Or is it who?" Hilda replied, trying to act innocently and keep her eyes from looking to the back room.

"You know very well that I am speaking of Richard," Zelda said. "Word has spread that he deserted his troop. Naturally I assumed that he came to see you."

"He did not desert," Hilda said indignantly. "He just popped over to see me."

"Hilda, dear," Zelda said. "His men are stationed in Pennsylvania. He does not have the means to just 'pop' over to see you, unless you've told him that—"

"I have done no such thing," Hilda said before Zelda could finish the thought. "But I am sure he is on his way back to the fighting."

Zelda sat her sister down so they could speak quietly, still unaware that there was a mortal in the adjoining room. "I am concerned," she continued. "There has been talk that he has been hinting around that you are not what you seem."

"Nonsense," Hilda said in a whisper. "If he were suspicious, he would have come to ask me directly."

"Hilda, you have always been a very trusting woman," Zelda said, lowering her voice to match her sister's, though the look on her face implied that she didn't know why they were talking so softly. "How many times has Drell promised to meet you and then stood you up?"

"Richard is different," Hilda said.

"Yes, he is," Zelda agreed. "He's mortal. And I think he has an agenda. I think he's planning to expose you and the rest of our family in the process."

"Nonsense," Hilda said.

"I don't think so," Zelda continued. "I've asked Mother to come—"

"How could you?" Hilda cried. "When are you going to finally understand that mother—"

A scream was heard from outside the house. It was so loud and so sudden that even Sabrina jumped when she heard it in the flashback. She watched as her aunts hurried from the house into the dark night.

"Mother, what have you done?" Hilda yelled as she saw her beau standing frozen. At first he just appeared to be standing extremely still, but as Sabrina looked closer, she noticed that he had a definite look of granite about him.

"You've turned him to stone," Zelda said. "Mother, do you think you might be acting just the least bit irrationally?"

"Better that he is stone than all of us being turned into mice," Sabrina's grandmother, Lydia, replied with a satisfied look in her eyes. "I caught him sneaking out the window. I can only imagine where he was going and what he was going to do."

"Exactly," Hilda said. "You can only imagine, because you do not know."

"Your sister has filled me in on the stories that have been spreading as a result of his words," Lydia said.

"But it's just rumors," her daughter replied.

"Hilda, we are living in a dangerous time," Zelda said, trying to calm her sister. "Gossip alone can cause us much trouble. Now, I'm sure once Mother comes up with a spell to make him forget—"

"I have the perfect spell right here," Lydia

interrupted, tapping on the statue. "I do not think he will be saying anything to anyone in his present form."

Hilda could not believe what she was hearing. "Mother, you can't!"

"I can and I shall," Lydia replied. "Now help me move him someplace less conspicuous."

Sabrina watched as her aunt ran back into their home. As the door closed behind her, the waviness returned and the fog rolled in, obscuring the picture. The flashback disappeared, leaving the two of them sitting alone with the statue in the small clearing. Sabrina couldn't help but notice that the statue still looked exactly as it had in the flashback. The poor man had been stuck here for over two hundred years.

"I can't believe that Grandmom—" Sabrina cut herself off. "No, actually, I *can* totally believe Grandmom would have done that, but I can't believe that Aunt Zelda wouldn't have made her change him back."

"Well, your aunt found a bunch of my stuff in his house and she jumped to the conclusion that he was gathering evidence to expose me as a witch," Hilda said somewhat indignantly.

"I'm sure there was a perfectly good explanation for why he had your stuff," Sabrina said, coming to Hilda's defense only a few hundred years too late for it to do any good.

"I'm sure there was too," Hilda said. "I just wish I could figure out what it was."

"And you still come out here to leave flowers at his statue after all this time?" Sabrina asked, surprised to learn this little tidbit about her aunt.

"Like clockwork," Hilda said. "Every ten years since he was statue-ized."

"Every *ten* years?" Sabrina asked.

"Well, it would be a little morbid to come *every* year," Hilda replied. "It *has* been over two centuries. At this point, it's become a tradition. I've pretty much gotten over him, especially since I'm having so much fun with Wayne."

"Speaking of whom," Sabrina said, remembering once again what a great day she had been having, "I had a meeting with President Banning today."

"Yes, he told me all about the scholarship," Hilda said in her still melancholy tone. "Congratulations."

This was not quite the reaction Sabrina had been hoping for, but she could understand that Hilda might not be in the best mood. Sabrina decided to hold off on telling her aunt about the rest of her great day until a better time. However, at this point, she was beginning to suspect that she was never going to be able to tell anyone about her great news.

"Why don't I just leave you alone for a bit,"

Sabrina said as she got up. "I have to find someone, anyway."

"Thanks," Hilda said, barely noticing her
niece's departure.

Sabrina quietly left the small grove so as not
to disturb her aunt any further. As soon as she
cleared the tree line, however, she forgot all
about her aunt.

"There you are," Christy Caldwell said in a
tone that seemed less than pleased.

"I've been looking all over for you," Sabrina
replied.

"Well, you weren't going to find me hiding in
the trees," Christy said.

The reporter was standing in the park dressed
in clothes that were much better suited to office
work than walking around in a park. Sabrina mar-
veled at how the woman's tall stiletto heels were
not sinking into the soft ground, and assumed
that it must take years of practice to maintain
one's balance like that. However Sabrina had no
real interest in adding that particular skill to her
résumé.

Christy took off, heading for the walking
trails. She did not wait to make sure that Sabrina
was following, which forced the young witch to
hurry along. The reporter moved at a fast pace,
which totally fit in with the way she stormed her
way through life.

"So where do we start?" Sabrina asked.

"I already have," was Christy's reply. "It's about time you got here."

"Mike didn't tell me exactly where you were going to be," Sabrina replied apologetically.

Christy stopped short, leading Sabrina to believe that everything this woman did was sudden and exact. "First he sticks me with an intern . . . ," the reporter started to say, but then trailed off, leaving the thought unfinished.

There was no way Sabrina had any intention of telling this woman about her good day. She would probably just ruin the mood entirely.

"Look," Christy said. "We've got a lot of ground to cover. Literally. I need you to start interviewing tourists in the park. Ask them the basics. Why they came. Their favorite park of the trail. That kind of thing. Then we're going to walk the trail, since I've never been on it before."

"It's really—" Sabrina started to say.

"I'm sure it is," Christy said, interrupting, with no interest in what Sabrina had to say. "But we don't have time to be tourists. After we walk the trail, we've got a bunch of research to do about the historical facts and such."

"I did a report on it in high school." Sabrina immediately regretted what she was saying the moment the words left her mouth.

"Well, isn't that darling?" the woman replied,

using a tone that obviously implied she didn't find it to be darling at all.

"I was just—" Sabrina started.

"I'm sure you were," the reporter interrupted again before allowing Sabrina to even make her point. "But we don't have time for chitchat. It's going to be a long afternoon."

And there went the statement Sabrina had dreaded hearing. She knew it meant that they would not be heading back to the office today and that she wouldn't have a chance to see Josh. One of the best days of her life was going to continue, and nobody was going to know anything about it.

"Stop daydreaming, Sabrina," Christy called to Sabrina. Christy had already walked about half a block before Sabrina had even noticed she had moved. "We've got a lot to do."

Chapter 3

"Nobody say a word," Sabrina said as soon as she walked through the door of the house she shared with her college roommates. "I have great news."

Roxie and Miles were sitting on the couch watching television while Morgan was fixing herself a snack. They had lived with Sabrina long enough to be familiar with her easily excited personality and pretty much continued what they were doing, only halfheartedly listening.

"Come on, I've been waiting all day to tell someone," she pleaded while taking off her jacket and moving over to the couch.

Roxie reluctantly turned off the television so that she and Miles could give her their full attention. Neither of them seemed too keen on missing the rest of the show they were watching. Being college students, there was an almost endless supply of soap operas, talk shows, and classic TV to keep them occupied between classes. At times even Sabrina was amazed by the junk she and her roommates would spend hours watching. Meanwhile Morgan moved from the kitchen to the couch to join in the conversation, leaving behind the snack she was making from some leftover food they had.

"Wow, I've been waiting so long to tell someone, I don't know where to begin," Sabrina said, sitting on the arm of the couch.

"Wherever you begin, I'd suggest getting to it," Roxie said. "Judge Judy was about to render her verdict, and we cut it off for you."

Knowing how seriously Roxie took being inconvenienced, Sabrina plunged ahead with her tale. Glossing over the A on her astronomy paper, she focused on telling them all about how her paper was accepted in the science annual. She had expected at least a smile of praise from Miles, but when he continued to look at her blank-faced, she moved on to her news about the alumni scholarship and the special supplement for the newspaper. When she was done, she was still met with the same looks that her roommates had at the start of her story. "Well?" she said.

"Isn't that nice," Morgan said in a slightly demeaning voice before heading upstairs to her room, picking up her snack along the way.

"Good job," Roxie halfheartedly added before picking up the remote and turning the TV back on. She had missed the judge's verdict, and the show had already moved on to the next case.

Miles just sat quietly on the couch and turned back to the TV. He didn't even bother to respond.

"That's it?" Sabrina asked incredulously. "I have the most amazing day of my life and that's all anyone can say?"

"It wasn't that amazing," Roxie said, eyes still glued to the television. "For you, that is."

Sabrina placed herself between her roommates and the TV. "What is that supposed to mean?"

"Nothing bad," Roxie quickly replied. "It's just that these kinds of things always happen to you. We've come to expect it by now."

"What kinds of things?" Sabrina asked, truly having no clue what her roommate was talking about. She had never been published in a science journal before, or received a scholarship.

"*Good* kinds of things," Roxie said, turning down the volume but still keeping the TV on. "They happen to you all the time. I'm not saying that you don't work hard, but you're always getting great grades, and stuff like this is always happening to you."

"Good things don't always happen to me," Sabrina said, almost apologetically.

"I've never seen you fail at anything except *Chick Chat*." Roxie was referring to the radio show that she and Sabrina had started together before Sabrina realized that she had no talent for radio. "And even then you went right out and got a job at the newspaper. Sabrina, you've written several articles, and you're only an intern."

"Sometimes you can be so negative," Sabrina said as she squeezed herself onto the couch between Roxie and Miles. "What do you think, Miles?"

"Well, she *is* right about you almost always getting good grades," he said, obviously trying to evade the conversation. Miles was well practiced at changing the subject because, being the only male in the house, he often found himself in the middle of these types of discussions. This time, however, there appeared to be something more behind his avoidance of the subject.

"But does that mean you can't be happy for me?" Sabrina asked.

"I'm happy for you," Miles said quickly. "But I'm not going to do cartwheels in the living room."

"I would have settled for a simple 'congratulations' or something," Sabrina said. "Especially for being in the science annual. I thought you, if anyone, would be happy for me."

"I am," Miles replied, looking trapped instead

of genuinely pleased. "But I'd be happier if I could get an article in the journal, instead of laughed out of the editor's office like I have been the last three times I submitted something. You'd think they'd welcome articles about the connection between alien sightings and celebrity appearances on *Who Wants to Be a Millionaire?* I mean, who are their phone-a-friends, anyway?"

"Oh, Miles, I'm sorry," Sabrina said.

"I'm not looking for pity," Miles replied.

Sabrina had been so excited about her news, she hadn't really thought about how it would have an impact on her friends. Miles was a student in the science department and did take his theories very seriously, though very few others did. Roxie was also into journalism, and Sabrina would always come home with news about her work on the paper. *But,* she realized, *just because they might be jealous doesn't mean they still can't be happy for me.*

"Look, I understand how you guys might not be as excited about these things as I am," Sabrina said. "But I do work very hard to get where I am."

"Right," they both said, although Sabrina couldn't tell if they were agreeing or being sarcastic. She assumed the worst, as the doorbell rang.

"Hey, if you two knew all the stuff I had to deal with, you wouldn't be so jealous," Sabrina said as she got up to open the door, since neither of her roommates budged from their places on the couch. She couldn't help but be a little upset with them. Of course they had no idea how difficult it was to be a good student when things like evil relatives suddenly popping up and casting spells on her and her aunts could really have an impact on her study habits.

As Sabrina crossed the room, she could hear Morgan starting back down the steps. Morgan was the type of popular girl who always assumed that when someone came to the door or called on the phone, it was for her. Sometimes, Sabrina envied that confidence. When someone came to the door for her, it seemed as if they were always bringing some kind of magical trouble. And here her friends thought she had such an easy life.

"If that's for me," Morgan said from her place on the stairs, "find out who it is before you let them in. I'm screening my visitors today."

Sabrina didn't bother to respond since she was used to Morgan's rather eccentric requests, even though she wasn't thrilled about being her roommate's answering service. Sabrina opened the front door to find the unlikely pair of Josh and Harvey waiting. "What are you two doing together?" she asked before she realized how she could have better phrased that question.

"We're only on the porch together," Josh said. "We came separately."

"I'm here to see Morgan," Harvey said as he passed Sabrina to enter the house without waiting for Sabrina to prescreen him. Sabrina let him go, figuring she really didn't care whether Morgan wanted to see Harvey.

"I'm here because I missed you at work today," Josh said. "Mike told me about the supplement. I'm sorry you're stuck working with Christy."

"Yes, but you're happy that I'm doing the article, right?" Sabrina asked pointedly as she showed him into the house. The question was very much for the benefit of her roommates over on the couch.

"Sure," he replied, knowing her well enough not to question the oddly phrased question. "I was expecting you'd be moving up quickly at the *Citizen*. Mike seems to like your work."

"You expected it?" she asked, almost as an accusation.

"Tread carefully," Roxie warned from her perch on the couch. "She's in a mood."

"What's she talking about?" he asked.

"Never mind," Sabrina replied. "You were saying?"

Josh suddenly developed that deer-trapped-in-the-headlights look. The worst part was, he had no idea why the "headlights" were aimed at him. "Well . . . ," he began cautiously. "You started doing those columns about college life so quickly after starting as an intern, I just assumed he'd move you on to bigger and better things."

"Because everything comes so easily to me?" Sabrina asked.

"That's not what I said," he replied. "But you do have a lucky—"

"Luck!" Sabrina blurted. "I work really hard!"

"I know you do," Josh was backpedaling, but not knowing where to go. "I didn't mean to say . . . It's just you do . . . Is there any way I can get out of this?"

"Fake a head injury and run for it," Harvey said. "It's worked for me in the past."

"What do you want?" Josh started.

"You be quiet," Ssabrina said to Josh and then looked at Harvey. "You come with me."

"Oooohhh, you're in trouble!" Roxie and Miles said in unison.

Giving up on Josh, Sabrina led Harvey back out to the porch and made sure the door was closed so that her roommates couldn't hear. Once that was confirmed, she quickly turned toward Harvey with a dangerous look in her eyes.

"Before you start yelling at me too," Harvey

said before she could speak, "Josh didn't say anything that would justify you jumping down his throat like that. Now since I'm not one to come to his rescue so easily, will you tell me what's bothering you?"

"I had an amazing day," Sabrina said, as if that was the answer to his question.

"You sure have a funny way of celebrating," he replied.

"That's just it," she said. "I was ready to celebrate but everyone else seemed to think that it was nothing special. Roxie even tried to say that I have it easy or something. If she only knew."

"Look, Sabrina, I know you work hard for things and deserve what you get," Harvey said carefully. "But you have to admit, some of us just have a harder time with school and stuff than you do. To us, your life looks pretty easy."

"But now that you know the truth," Sabrina said, hinting at the one thing he knew about her than none of her other mortal friends did, "you know how difficult it is for me to hide my secret?"

"Well, yeah," Harvey said. "But what an amazing secret. I mean, if I had your powers . . ."

"Not you, too," Sabrina said, resigning herself to the fact that none of her friends truly appreciated just how difficult her life really was.

"You know, I banged my head earlier in

hockey practice . . . ," Harvey started to say as he backed away toward the front door.

"Don't you dare move," she said. "Do you or do you not think that my life is easy?"

"You do seem to have your fair share of inter-esting—"

"What is your answer?" she asked again, coming across very much like the judge that Roxie and Miles were watching on the other side of the door.

There was a very long pause as Harvey chose his words carefully. "Are you sure you wouldn't rather have this conversation with someone you haven't turned into a geek, a frog, a ninja, a gun-slinger—"

"I get the point," she interrupted.

"And a pregnant teen," he added one last one for good measure.

"I do want your opinion," she replied. "You've always been honest with me, even when I couldn't be honest with you."

"Okay, then," he replied. "Yes, I think that even though you do work hard, and even though having magic can be weird at times, your life is easier than some of the people you know."

"I can't believe it!" she yelled. "I thought at least you would have some kind of an idea what I'm going through. How can you stand there and tell me that I have an easy life?"

Sabrina was so mad that instead of waiting for an answer, she made herself disappear.

"I'd say being able to disappear from your problems is a plus," Harvey said.

Chapter 4

"I can't believe my friends sometimes," Sabrina said through clenched teeth as she reappeared in the middle of her aunts' living room.

"Alert! Alert!" Salem yelled from his place on the sofa table. "Angry college student! Alert!"

Sabrina turned on the cat. "I swear, you don't know how lucky you are, Salem. Nobody ever expects anything from you."

"And yet that still doesn't make up for the fact that I'm plagued by hair balls and my bathroom is inconveniently located in a high traffic area of the house," he retorted.

Zelda hurried down the steps to find out what the commotion was about. "Hi, sweetie," she said to her niece. "I heard our early warning system go off. What's Salem talking about?"

Sitting Sabrina down on the couch, Zelda tried to shoo Salem out of the room, but the stubborn cat had no intention of going anywhere. His philosophy of life tended to be that it was so much easier to eavesdrop when he was a part of the conversation.

"I was having this really great day . . . ," Sabrina started.

"Oh, I know," Zelda said. "I heard all about your paper being accepted into the science annual from Professor Hall, and Hilda told me about the scholarship. I am so thrilled!"

"At last," Sabrina said. "Someone who's actually happy for my accomplishments."

"Well, you know what they say, dear," Zelda replied, "'The only thing you have to do to make me happy is come home at the end of the day.' Although I would like it if you did come home more often."

"Just couldn't help slipping that in, could you?" Sabrina asked.

"Don't worry, Sabrina," Salem added. "I like you being gone so that I can have your old room all to myself."

The two witches turned to give him the evil eye, but didn't put any real magic behind the look. They turned their backs on him, ignoring another one of his snide comments.

"But the best part," Sabrina continued, "is that I'm cowriting a special supplement for the *Citizen*."

"Oh, that's wonderful," Zelda said. "I always knew you were destined for greatness."

"But you understand how hard I work for it, right?" Sabrina asked for the sake of clarification. "Especially in light of some family traits that could be seen as gifts but are more often a hindrance?"

"Sabrina, I thought you had gotten over that years ago," Zelda said. "I know it's difficult, but being a witch should not interfere with your mortal life."

"That's just the point," Sabrina said. "It *is* difficult and I *do* manage to keep it from interfering as best as I can, but you and Aunt Hilda are the only people who know that. Even Harvey, who knows my secret, thinks I have it easy."

"Sabrina, it's not like you to be so insecure," Zelda said.

"Sounds just like her to me," Salem interjected.

"Salem!" Both witches yelled in unison.

"Okay, okay, I'm going." The cat dropped from his perch on the table and started to leave the room. But in typical Salem fashion, he didn't actually *leave* the room,. He just made it look that way so he could eavesdrop from the hall.

"Look," Sabrina said, "I know we've been through this before, but I just wish my friends could understand how difficult it is to be me.

They all think I have the perfect life and all I want is for them to see that it's not."

"I wish I could help, honey," Zelda said. "But since the Witches' Council has recently gone and closed every loophole in the book that covered witches telling mortals about their powers, there's just nothing we can do."

"How strange for Other Realm bureaucracy to work against me," Sabrina said sarcastically.

Both witches could hear Salem's little giggle from behind them. They had known the cat long enough now to have expected that he hadn't gone very far. Since there was no use telling him to go away, they just continued to ignore him.

"Truth be told," Zelda said, getting herself into parental-moral mode, "everyone has difficulties in their lives. You should learn to appreciate your magic more and look at it as a gift and not as the hindrance you believe it to be. You shouldn't worry about what effect it has on how your mortal friends look at your accomplishments. It's part of who you are."

"Thank you, Aunt *Glinda*," Sabrina said, making a *Wizard of Oz* reference. "But I guess what you're saying does make sense."

"It's what I'm here for," she replied.

"Do you mind if I hang out here for a while?" Sabrina asked. "I don't feel like going home yet."

"Sabrina, you know you're always welcome here," Zelda said. "And it's nice to see you visiting without bringing your laundry."

Unfortunately Zelda spoke too soon because before she had even finished her sentence, a point from Sabrina's finger had magically transported her dirty laundry to the house.

"Then again," Zelda added, seeing the pile, "it's nice that you can be consistent about some things."

"Thanks, Aunt Zelda," Sabrina said as she picked up her clothes. "I do feel a little better."

"Glad to be of service," Zelda replied before heading back up the stairs to her room.

Sabrina continued down the hall into the laundry room with her clothes. Not surprisingly, Salem chose to follow coming up right on her heels. "Who are you kidding?" he said from the area around her feet. "You never learn your lesson that easily."

Sabrina ignored that cat as she placed her whites into the washing machine and turned the setting to hot. As she reached for detergent, Salem used his springlike legs to hop up onto a nearby shelf so he could talk to her over the noise of the washer.

"Come on, I know you're trying to figure out some way to teach your friends a valuable lesson," he said to her. "We've been through this enough times before. Do I really need to convince you to admit the truth to me?"

"Salem, leave me alone," she replied, pouring in the soap.

"I know you want to." He kept pushing in the childlike way he tended to revert to from time to time. "And I know the perfect spell."

Sabrina closed the lid to the washer, stalling for time so she could come up with a reason to convince Salem—and herself—not to turn to magic to solve her problem. She couldn't help but think that Salem had always tended to know the *imperfect* spell whenever she had listened to him in the past.

"My Magic CD-ROM is back at my place," she said, coming up with the best excuse she could. "And I don't feel like going home right now."

"Then it's a good thing that your old Magic Book is still in your room here," Salem said as he hopped back down to the floor and headed for the stairs.

He didn't even have to look back to know that she was following him. As Salem bounded up the kitchen stairs, he could hear Sabrina's soft footsteps behind him. A small smile came over his face, knowing he was about to have at least an afternoon's worth of entertainment, which beat watching *When Animals Attack* on the all-animal-themed cable channel.

"Okay, what's the spell this time?" she asked as she entered her old bedroom. Sabrina knew that whenever she took Salem's advice she was almost always doomed to fail, but somehow the temptation always proved too great for her to say no.

Salem leaped up onto the bed, finding a spot somewhere between all of the cat toys he had strewn about. "It's called a See-Things-Through-My-Eyes spell. And it lets your friends see how life is through your eyes."

"This isn't one of those disgustingly literal spells, is it?" Sabrina asked cautiously, remembering numerous past spells that had taken puns just a step too far. "Because I like the eyes I have and I don't want them to be removed, switched, or given to my friends in any way."

Salem gave a little chuckle because he knew that her concern was warranted. "No, this is one of the old ones. It was written before witches started getting creative with their wordplay."

"Are you sure?" she asked.

"Check it out yourself," he replied, pointing a paw in the direction of the Magic Book.

Sabrina walked over to the stand where the book was kept, blew the thin layer of dust off it, and began flipping through the pages. Over the past year she had been casting spells by using the Magic CD-ROM that she'd gotten when she'd started college, and had only used her old book once or twice.

"Here it is," she said as she found the page. "The See-Things-Through-My-Eyes spell. 'Guaranteed to make your friend know what it's like to live your life. Promotes a better understanding and deeper friendship.' Well, that sounds harmless enough."

"Of course it does," Salem said. "When have I ever given you bad . . . never mind."

"Wait a second," Sabrina said, still reading. "It says here that once the spell has run its course, the subject of the spell will forget everything."

"Keep reading, O Quick-to-Judge," Salem prodded her along.

"Oh, I see." Sabrina turned the page and continued. "But it says 'They will be left with a better understanding of what it's like to be in the spellcaster's shoes.' Let's get started."

"Don't forget the fine print," Salem reminded her.

"I'm not in high school anymore," she said again, thinking back to the myriad of spells gone awry because she had hurried through a reading of the instructions. "I know better now."

Sabrina skimmed down the page reading the many lines of fine print. Mostly there were warnings that did not apply to her situation, such as: *Do not use on trolls*, and *Cannot be performed by witches over one thousand years old*. Then there were rules that Sabrina couldn't imagine applied to any situation, such as: *Do not recite while standing on one foot in a hailstorm wearing pink leopard print galoshes*.

There were, however, two very important rules that she noted. The first was that the spell would wear off in twenty-four hours, which made perfect sense to Sabrina. The second rule—the "Rule of the Ones"—made no sense to her whatsoever. The rule stated: *The Spell Can Only Be Performed by One Witch Once and Only on One Friend*.

"But that doesn't help," she said to Salem. "I want *all* of my friends to understand what it's like to be me."

"I guess that just means we have to be a little creative," Salem said.

"Maybe we can just change a few words of the spell around," Sabrina said, reading over the page.

Why does she always listen to me? Salem silently asked himself. *The question is: Should I stop her from making what will probably be a huge mistake, or should I just let her continue? Oh, who am I kidding?*

Salem hopped up to look over Sabrina's shoulder as she read the spell to herself, studying it for the proper wording.

With nothing to lose
My life, dreams, and lies,
The one friend I have
Can see though my eyes.

"Why do witches always use such crazy sentence construction?" Sabrina asked. "I swear, an English teacher would have a field day marking this book up in red pencil."

"It keeps the spells from accidentally being chanted in everyday conversation," Salem replied. "I mean, what are the odds you're going to say those words in that order on a normal day?"

"Good point," Sabrina said. "It looks like it should be easy enough for me to change around. Stand back, Salem."

For safety's sake, Salem hid under the bed.

Sabrina took a step back from the book and chanted.

"With nothing to lose,
My life, dreams, and lies,
Every friend I have,
Can see though my eyes."

She gave a little point at her eyes as the spell had instructed and immediately felt a tingle. She assumed that the spell had worked. A quick glance into her mirror revealed that her eyes were still blue, so by all appearances she assumed that everything had gone well.

"Is this one of those immediate spells or are we going to have to wait before the effects can be seen?" she asked Salem as he crawled covered in dust out from under the bed .

Okay, maybe someone should dust under there, she thought.

Salem shook off the dust, embarrassed to do one of the patented "dog" moves, but he knew it was better than bathing the dust off with his tongue. "You probably won't see any results until morning," he said. "But, then again, if you *really* want your friends to have to live your life of hiding magic, you shouldn't even see anything at all."

"What a cool spell," she said as she picked him up to give him a little hug and dust him off. "Thanks, Salem. I totally feel better."

Sabrina put Salem down back on the bed among his toys and practically skipped out of the room to check on her laundry—the Spellmans had a magical washer and dryer that always got the job done quickly.

"And yet, I can't shake this really bad feeling," Salem said to himself as soon as Sabrina was out of earshot.

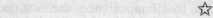

Chapter 5

Sabrina had trouble sleeping since she was so excited to see what would happen in the morning. The excitement over watching her friends hide their magic from her and one another while only she knew what was going on was too much to allow her to get any rest. She did manage to nod off about two o'clock, but she woke up again at five thirty. Not wanting to lie in bed thinking over all the possibilities, Sabrina got up to get ready for what promised to be a very fun day.

While Sabrina was getting dressed in the bathroom, her roommates were waking up with new powers that they believed they'd had their entire lives. But when Sabrina came out into the living room, she was the one who received the unexpected shock. She watched as Roxie levitated two pancakes across the room to her plate.

"Morning, Sabrina," Roxie said in an unusually chipper voice.

"Good morning," Sabrina responded tentatively. "Making a little breakfast?"

"Yeah," Roxie replied as her knife and fork cut her pancakes on their own. "Oh, you know what would be good? Sausage!" Roxie gave a little point, and the breakfast meat appeared on her plate.

Well, part of the spell worked, Sabrina thought. *Roxie has magical powers. But why isn't she hiding them from me?*

"Hey, would you like some pancakes?" Roxie asked, her finger poised for pointing. "They're coming out especially good today."

"No, thanks," Sabrina said, her mind working overtime trying to figure out what was going on. "One bite and I blow up like a balloon."

Just then an explosion came from Miles's room.

Roxie didn't even react.

Sabrina hurried across the living room but by the time she had reached Miles's door, he was already coming out, looking none the worse for wear.

"What was that?" Sabrina asked, peeking back into his bedroom, which looked unusually immaculate.

"Oh, just another experiment in finding other dimensions," he replied casually. "I really blew a hole in the house that time."

Once again Sabrina looked back into the room, but nothing looked out of place. In fact, it was cleaner than she had ever seen it before.

"Where's the hole?" she asked.

"I fixed it, naturally," Miles replied as he strolled over to the kitchen.

As if to complete the cast, Morgan came down the stairs in a stunning blue sequin dress, carrying her schoolbooks. She gave a twirl once she reached the center of the room to show off the outfit to her roommates. It was as if she was expecting applause. Morgan liked being the center of attention, and she was certainly getting some attention in that wild dress.

"You're not wearing *that* to class, are you?" Sabrina asked.

"Too flashy," Morgan replied. "How about this?" She waved her hand in front of her body, and the blue sequins turned to red velvet. The color may have been more appropriate for day wear, but the outfit was way over-the-top for collegiate attire. Not to mention how uncomfortable the three-inch high heels must have been. But then, Sabrina noticed that Morgan was floating ever so slightly off the floor so that she wasn't putting any weight on her feet and doing irreparable damage to her ankles.

"Did you suddenly sign up for a ballroom dance class?" Sabrina asked. "Because the blue would probably be cooler to wear."

"No, silly. This is what I always wear to class," Morgan replied before shooting a look at Roxie. "Why dress in the drab uniform of jeans and a T-shirt when you can whip up any outfit you want?"

Knowing that the implied insult was directed at Roxie, Sabrina waited for her roommate's usual biting and witty response. However, rather than a verbal barb, Roxie pointed her finger and suddenly Morgan was dressed in a chicken suit with her face sticking out of the mouth.

Flapping her arm/wings wildly, Morgan fired back, leaving Roxie in tattered rags. Sabrina had been used to the two of them throwing insults back and forth, but she wasn't ready for them to be throwing magic. She had to duck to make sure that a wayward spell did not bring her into the battle. Realizing her own spell had gone amazingly wrong, Sabrina ran back to her room and shut the door.

As soon as the latch on the door clicked, Sabrina chanted:

"Because my roommates' powers grew,
Of this spell I must undo."

Sabrina pointed her finger back toward the living room and took a deep breath. Opening the door she could see that the girls were still trading magical insults, with Roxie dressed like a clown and Morgan outfitted in something resembling a miniature circus tent. Meanwhile Miles was floating three feet above the couch, watching the entertaining display from a safe distance.

Sabrina closed the door once again.

"Okay, don't panic," Sabrina said to herself as she began to pace around the room. "The undo spell didn't work. . . . I could try another spell to counteract this one. But that could just make things worse. . . . Maybe if I just wait it out. . . . No, who knows what could happen? . . . Okay, maybe this time I'll just cut to the chase and go to my aunts for help."

Sabrina pointed at herself, intending to be transported to her aunts' house, but she didn't move an inch.

"This is not good," she said as she pointed again and found herself still in the same spot. "Oh, this is *so* not good."

Not giving up, Sabrina pointed at her jacket, trying to will it to come to her, but it refused to move as well. Furiously, she pointed her finger around the room, trying to will different objects to move, disappear, or change color—anything. Every item she pointed at refused to cooperate.

"Maybe a spell will work," Sabrina said to herself.

"Because I'm in a lot of trouble,
Bring my aunts here, on the double."

Nothing.

She grabbed her jacket and ran back through the living room, ignoring Morgan, dressed as a Goth chick, and Roxie, dressed as a cheerleader, were both pointing to Miles and making him spin in circles.

"Roxie, please take notes for me in class," Sabrina said as she headed for the front door without stopping. "I've got to run a quick errand. I shouldn't be long."

Once outside, Sabrina took a deep breath and began the trek to her aunts' house. She had hardly gotten off the stoop before the trip was immediately halted.

"Hi," a familiar voice said into her right ear.

"Aaacchh!" She jumped in shock and nearly fell off the bottom step.

"Sorry, I didn't mean to scare you," Josh said, although his giggles told her otherwise. "I just popped over to say hi."

Sabrina didn't reply because her mind was busy registering the fact that yet another one of her friends now had her magic powers and was proudly using them out in the open. This one was even worse because they were quite literally out in the open. It was one thing for Miles, Roxie, and Morgan to work spells in the house, but a group of kids were running by the moment Josh had appeared. He wasn't hiding his magic from anyone.

"But I've got to get to work now, so bye," he said, and disappeared again.

"It's a good thing my friends are using their powers for good reasons," Sabrina said sarcastically.

Things were officially getting out of hand. Unfortunately Sabrina realized too late that she should have asked Josh to zap her home. Afraid to go back inside and get caught in the middle of the magical argument, Sabrina continued on foot to the nearest bus stop. *Not a great time for my car to be in the shop,* she thought. Sabrina hoped public transportation would get her to her aunts' house in a hurry.

Walking along the perimeter of campus, she noticed several odd sites. An elderly woman was walking her purple dog, and several boys were catching extremely major air on their skateboards. She recognized the woman as the wife of one of the college professors. The dog, Sabrina recalled, used to be a pure white poodle. Trying to avoid the obvious, Sabrina kept walking until she could no longer ignore the signs. The road in front of her ended abruptly, and in its place was a deep chasm about a hundred feet across. "That wasn't there yesterday," Sabrina said aloud.

"I'm afraid I may have done that," the woman with the purple dog said as she came up beside Sabrina. "The old magic just isn't what it used to be."

"This is *not* good," Sabrina said.

"No problem at all," the woman said. "I'll fix it."

With a wave of the woman's hand, the ground began to shake and the chasm closed, leaving the sidewalk back in place as if nothing had ever happened.

"There," the woman said, proud of her accomplishment. "I've still got a few years left in these old hands."

"Thanks," Sabrina said, although her mind was a thousand miles away.

Continuing to the bus stop, Sabrina couldn't help but notice that the sky kept changing color. First blue, then red, then green, and blue once again. She looked around, but no one else seemed to notice anything odd going on above them. Sabrina hoped she was the only one seeing it, but figured that she couldn't be that lucky. Obviously to everyone else, it was just a normal occurrence. Her spell must have affected the entire college.

When she finally reached the bus stop, the sky was back to being blue and no other magical happenings got in her way. When the bus arrived, she quickly boarded and took a seat in the back—she was the only one on the bus. Sabrina had been on this bus a few times before and did not remember it ever being this empty, no matter what time of day she had been on it. As she tried to figure out the significance of the empty bus, the driver pulled out into the street and then took off into the air.

Sabrina was slammed back in her seat as the bus lifted off the ground, rising higher and higher at an incredible speed. Then, for no apparent reason, the driver turned the wheel sharply and the bus started rolling over in the air. As Sabrina was flung out of her seat, she grabbed on to the nearest bar and tried not to bang into anything. All the while, her only thought was about how much she wished the thing had seat belts. The driver, however, was resting comfortably in his own seat as if he were just heading down the street instead of looping through the air.

"Oh, yeah," Sabrina said to herself as the driver/pilot finally righted the bus. "I am definitely going to miss my stop."

Sabrina looked out the large window to the town below and could see that they had just crossed over the boarder between Boston and

Westbridge. Looking ahead a little, she could see her aunts' house coming up below. Sabrina grabbed the pull cord to let the driver know that her stop was approaching. As soon as the bell rang, the bus dropped to the ground.

Fearing that the bus was about to become flatter than Roxie's pancakes, Sabrina braced for impact. Instead of crashing into the street, the bus slowed about a good twenty feet above the ground and came down gently.

"Collins Road," the driver announced as the doors to the bus opened.

Sabrina shakily got to her feet, still holding on to the bar for fear of the bus suddenly lurching forward. Once she got her balance, Sabrina hurried onto the street. She could see her aunts' house only a few doors away. Upon hearing the driver gun the engine, she turned in time to watch the bus shoot back up into the sky. "I really hope my aunts are home," she said as she started for the house.

Chapter 6

"**A**unt Zelda! Aunt Hilda!" Sabrina hollered as she burst into the Spellman home. "We've got a major problem! And I mean *major*!"

"What? What is it?" Hilda asked as she rushed in from the kitchen. "Did a swarm of fairies take over the coffeehouse?"

"Um, I'm going with 'no' on that one," Sabrina said, noticing how much happier Hilda seemed than the last time she had seen her aunt back at the statue of Richard Locksley.

"Good," Hilda said with a sigh of relief. "The place was such a mess the last time it happened, I had to hire a fleet of Magical Maintenance Men to clean it up. And you know how much I hate to do that."

"What's wrong?" Zelda asked as she hurried into the room.

"I cast a spell," Sabrina said, heading over to the couch but feeling too tense to sit. "And now all my friends have magic and I've lost my powers."

There was an incredibly long silence while her aunts looked at each other. Sabrina braced herself for the lecture of her lifetime, but was more than willing to listen as long as her aunts could help her figure out how to reverse the spell.

"Sabrina, you should sit down," Zelda said in a soothing voice, sitting on the couch. "We thought you had gotten over this years ago."

"Gotten over what?" Sabrina asked as she reluctantly sat down.

"Losing your powers," Hilda added, then prodded her niece's memory. "When you turned sixteen."

"What are you talking about?" Sabrina asked as she got that sinking feeling in her stomach. This was definitely not the kind of talking-to she had expected to get from her aunts.

"Oh dear, I was afraid this would happen," Zelda said. "You handled things so well when you were in high school. The stress of being in college now must have caused a little snap. Nothing to worry about."

Hilda spoke slowly and loudly, as if each word were a sentence unto itself. "Do. You. Remember. Losing. Your. Powers?"

"No," Sabrina said softly, playing along, hoping to find out what was happening and how invariably she was responsible for making it happen.

"Think hard, Sabrina," Zelda said. "It happened on the morning of your sixteenth birthday. The day you found out you were half-witch."

"Of course I remember that," Sabrina said, without having to search her memory files. "It was the most important day in my life. But I didn't *lose* my powers, I gained them."

"This is worse than I thought," Zelda said, getting up to pace, since now *she* was too tense to sit.

Hilda took her sister's place on the couch beside Sabrina. "Let's try this," she said. "Sabrina, who is your mother?"

"Diana Becker," she replied.

"Very good," Hilda said, patting her niece on the hand. "And is she a witch or a mortal?"

"Mortal?" Sabrina replied tentatively.

"Yes," Hilda practically cheered. "And where is she right now?"

"In Peru," Sabrina replied, more sure of herself.

"Doing what?" Zelda eagerly jumped in.

"Digging up bones on an archaeological site," Sabrina proudly answered.

"No!" both her aunts said as all their excitement immediately deflated.

"She's not?" Sabrina asked.

"No," Zelda replied. "She doesn't need to *dig* anything. She's using her mortal powers to recreate life in the Mesozoic era."

"*Mortal powers*? Okay, let me get this straight," Sabrina said, piecing together the information. "What you're telling me is that mortals have magic powers, and witches . . . don't?"

"Now she's got it!" Hilda exclaimed.

"Oh, this is bad on so many levels," Sabrina said.

"Not really," Hilda replied. "We manage to get along fairly well without magic. Thanks to the Black Magic Market."

"Isn't black magic bad?" Sabrina asked.

"No, silly," Hilda replied. "Just fake. Slightly above sleight-of-hand tricks."

"Okay, I know this isn't going to make any sense to you." Sabrina motioned for Zelda to join them on the couch. "But none of what you said is really supposed to be true."

Her aunts looked equally concerned and confused.

"On my sixteenth birthday I did find out that I was half-witch and had magical powers," Sabrina said. "Just like both of you, and my dad, and the rest of the Spellman family. We're witches and *we* have the magic. But I cast a spell that obviously went wrong, and now the world is all topsy-turvy and everything is upside down and backward. Now I need both of you to help me figure a way out of this."

Once again, her aunts just stared at each other.

"Sabrina, it's quite normal for half-mortals to have trouble coping with the loss of their powers," Zelda said, unable to believe what her niece was telling her.

Frustrated by the fact that her aunts refused to listen to her, Sabrina tried to take a hint from Hilda and change her own tactics. "Do you mind if I ask you both some questions?" Sabrina asked.

"Sure, honey," Zelda said, looking at her sister, who was nodding her head in return. "Whatever you want to know."

Using logic, Sabrina pieced together a list of questions hoping to jog her aunts' memories of having magic. "How old are you?" she asked.

"Now, you know it's rude to ask a lady's age," Hilda jokingly replied.

Zelda, however, took the question much more seriously. "We're in our thirties. Don't you remember the surprise party we threw for Hilda on her last birthday?"

Sabrina remembered the party distinctly. However she remembered it as a celebration of her aunt's 650th birthday. For a moment Sabrina began to think that maybe her aunts were right and she was the one who was confused.

"Okay, how about this." Sabrina moved on to to the next question. "Why did my parents send me to stay with you?"

Sabrina knew the right answer was so that they could teach her how to use her magic, but she wanted to know what her aunts would say.

"Well, since your father is stationed in France in the foreign service," Zelda said, dashing Sabrina's hope that he was on Pluto, as he was the last time they had spoken, "and your mother is in Peru, it was only natural that we take you in."

"But is there some specific reason why I can't visit my mother?" Sabrina prodded.

"Yes," Hilda replied. "Because since you don't have magic to protect you, they were worried a dinosaur would step on you."

"Why did you think you couldn't visit her?" Zelda asked.

"Because she'd turn into a ball of wax," Sabrina replied, with just about all of her energy drained from her body at learning just how badly her spell had gone wrong. At this point she was beginning to hope she was making everything up and her aunts were right.

"Maybe you should go up to your room and rest," Zelda suggested.

"Yes, that should do the trick," Hilda eagerly agreed.

Realizing that she was getting nowhere with

her aunts, Sabrina reluctantly decided to do as they said and head for her old bedroom. However, rest was the last thing on her mind. She was hoping to find an answer in the Magic Book. As Hilda and Zelda watched her go upstairs, their concern for her continued to grow.

"This is not good," Hilda said, stating the obvious. "I thought we were home free when she got out of high school."

"I know," Zelda said. "I guess we underestimated. Do you think we should leave her alone? There's no telling what she might do."

"You're right," Hilda said, heading for the stairs. "She's dealing with a lot right now."

The aunts hurried upstairs, but when they got to Sabrina's room, they found it empty. Standing in the hall, they heard a frustrated sigh coming from the linen closet. Tentatively, they walked toward it and opened the door to find their niece standing with her foot tapping angrily.

"Sabrina, dear," Zelda said with even more concern than she had downstairs. "Why are you standing in our linen closet?"

"I was trying to get to the Other Realm," Sabrina said.

"What other realm?" Zelda asked, showing her niece out into the hallway.

"Where the Witches' Council is," Sabrina replied.

"You mean Hoboken?" Hilda asked. "You can't get to New Jersey from our linen closet."

"And what do you want with that bureaucratic bunch of busybodies, anyway?" Zelda asked.

"Wait, you mean there still is a Witches' Council?" Sabrina asked, excited by the first piece of positive news since she had woken up this morning.

"Of course. Who do you think keeps witches protected from mortals' magic?" Zelda asked. "If mortals found out that witches really existed, there's no telling what they would do. The Council does their best to cover up evidence of witches and help them pretend to lead magical lives."

"I just wish they could do it without getting all in our business," Hilda said. "It's like they're always watching. It's worse than those reality TV shows. At least with those you have a chance to win a prize or a fabulous trip somewhere. Granted you usually have to eat a bug or something."

"I think I do need that rest," Sabrina said. "I'm going to lie down. But before I do, I just have one more question. It's about our toaster. Does it magically transport our mail, or is it only used for heating breakfast foods?"

"Would you like us to sit with you while you rest?" Zelda offered by way of her answer.

"No, I'll be fine," Sabrina said as she went into her old room and shut the door behind her.

Once in her room, she saw Salem lying on the bed. "Salem, you'll never believe what's going on," she said.

The cat just stared at her. For the second time since walking into the house, Sabrina began to think that she might actually be crazy and that her aunts were telling the truth. Maybe it *was* possible that she had made everything up and she really had lost her powers when she turned sixteen.

"Salem?" she asked, a note of terror in her voice. "I can't do this alone. Please tell me you can still speak?!"

"Oh, thank heaven," he said. "Finally someone who knows I can talk." The cat jumped up into her arms, having never been so happy to see her before in his life. He actually purred with excitement, which was a typical cat behavior that he very rarely performed.

"What's wrong?" she asked as she put him down on the bed.

Just then, they heard a soft knocking on the door. As they turned, Zelda opened the door and poked her head inside. "Sabrina, are you okay?" she asked. "I thought I heard you talking to someone."

Sabrina looked at Salem, who was shaking his

head frantically from side to side. "I was just saying to myself how lucky I was to have such wonderful aunts," Sabrina said. "Thank you for taking care of me."

"That's what we're here for," Zelda replied with a concerned smile on her face. "You get some rest."

"Okay," Sabrina said as she waited while her aunt slowly pulled the door closed.

As soon as she heard her aunt's footsteps softly fade away, she turned to the cat. He was sitting on her bed looking like he was about to explode. "What's going on?" she whispered.

"Some magic gone horribly awry, I'd say," Salem replied. "I woke up this morning to Zelda speaking baby talk to me like I was some dumb pet cat. When I asked her what she was doing, she nearly fainted. Then she started blaming Hilda for playing a practical joke and pretending that I could speak. Hilda told her that she didn't know anything about a joke and said that Zelda was crazy if she thought I was speaking. Then they started fighting. I haven't spoken since."

"Okay, then," Sabrina said. "Just to recap. I cast a spell so that every one of my friends would know what it was like to live my life. As it turns out, the spell went horribly wrong—"

"Imagine that," Salem jumped in.

"And instead of affecting every one of my

friends," she continued, "it's apparently affected *everyone* in Boston."

"Obviously, you haven't seen the news," Salem said.

"Don't tell me they reported that suddenly everyone has magical powers?" Sabrina nearly pleaded with the cat as if he had any control over the answer.

"Not quite," he replied. "It was just business as usual. Except for the fact that the reporters kept zapping themselves all over the globe to report on world news."

Sabrina's heart sank a little lower. "Okay, then, I broke the world. I gave mortals magic powers. But why did witches lose their powers?"

Neither of them having an answer, Salem and Sabrina just stared at each other for a moment. Both of them searched their memory banks for a time when a spell had backfired worse than the current one. Sure, they had gotten Westbridge stuck in the 1960s, set a dinosaur loose on the town, and accidentally turned many of Sabrina's friends into animals at one time or another. But they had never managed anything on a global level.

It was Salem who finally broke the silence. "That was one *big* spell you cast."

Chapter 7

☆

☆

"I'm drawing a total blank," Sabrina said after a half hour of trying to come up with a plan to get them out of this mess. "We are going to be trapped in Bizarro World forever."

Things were further complicated by the fact that, since they no longer had magic, the Spellmans no longer had a Magic Book. There was absolutely nothing in Sabrina's old bedroom that was going to help them solve their problem. Add to that the fact that her aunts were powerless, the Witches' Council was in Hoboken, Salem couldn't speak to anyone but Sabrina, and they had the makings for absolutely nothing.

"This is kind of like those *Star Trek* episodes that take place in a mirror universe," Salem said. "Where everything is opposite of the reality they're used to."

"All right then, my little Trekker," Sabrina

began, "how do we get out of this alternate universe we're stuck in?"

"We need to approach this logically," Salem said. "When I was plotting to take over the world, the first thing we did was reconnaissance. We learned as much as we could about a place before we tried to take it over."

"But you failed and were sentenced to a hundred years as a cat," Sabrina reminded him.

"Okay, there were a few problems with the plan," the feline admitted. "But let's not dwell on that. Which brings me to the question of why am I still a cat?"

"Obviously you weren't affected because you were with me when I cast the spell," Sabrina said. "But you're right, we do need more information. I'm going down to talk to my aunts. You wait here."

"That's about all I can do," he said as she headed for the door. "When you come back, bring a can of tuna or something. Zelda insists on feeding me dry cat food. Blech."

"Salem, I think we have a few more pressing things to worry about," Sabrina whispered as she opened her bedroom door.

"You'll change your mind when your only partner in crime drops dead from hunger," he whispered back, and Sabrina shut the door behind her.

Heading downstairs, Sabrina's mind was swimming with questions. As she slowly came down off the stairs, she nearly ran into a strange man who appeared right in front of her in the foyer.

"Sabrina, how have you been?" he asked, giving her an excited hug hello as if he hadn't seen her in a while.

She hugged him back, having no idea who he was but noticing something slightly familiar about his face. Sabrina searched her memory bank for any friends or members of the huge Spellman family that this stranger could be. In the years since she had come to live with her aunts, she had met many, many new people from the Other Realm. Then she realized that since he'd used magic to pop in, he must be a mortal. And Sabrina was sure he was no mortal she had ever met. "I'm fine," she said tentatively, not knowing when this person thought he had last seen her. "And you?"

"Never been better," he said, moving into the living room and making himself comfortable on the couch. "I had a great trip. Can you get your aunt for me?"

Sabrina reasoned that since he seemed so at home in the Spellman house, combined with the fact that he had given her such a warm hug, he must be a good friend of her aunts. Obviously this strange man had been here often. Of course, she had no idea where he had been on his "trip," but she had way more important things to worry about. Sabrina turned to head out of the room in search of her aunt. The only problem was that she didn't know which one to get.

Luckily both of her aunts were in the kitchen. The way they stopped talking as soon as Sabrina stepped into the room led her to assume the discussion had been about her. Naturally she couldn't blame them, since they were only concerned for her well-being and she was acting strangely as far as they could tell.

"We have a guest," Sabrina said, hoping that one of her aunts had been expecting the strange, yet slightly familiar, man in the living room.

"Who is it?" Zelda asked, dashing her niece's optimism immediately.

"It's a surprise," Sabrina said cryptically, since she really couldn't say anything else.

"Oh, I *love* surprises." Hilda hopped up from her chair, hurrying to the living room with her sister and niece following slowly behind.

"How are you feeling?" Zelda asked her niece while placing a hand on Sabrina's forehead in the universally accepted method of checking for a temperature. Sabrina couldn't figure out what having a temperature had to do with memory loss, but she wasn't going to complain.

"Much better," she replied. "I think I must have gotten hold of some bad Black Market Magic. But everything is slowly starting to come back—"

"Richard!" Hilda yelled as she saw the man on the couch. "You're back from the seventeen hundreds! How was your trip?"

Suddenly Sabrina knew exactly who the mysterious stranger was. It was no wonder that she hadn't recognized him, since the last time she had seen him he was a statue in the middle of Boston Common. Obviously when the witches and the mortals switched places, her grandmother's spell had worn off and Aunt Hilda's former boyfriend was freed from his imprisonment.

"That's the surprise guest?" Zelda asked with an obvious note of disappointment in her voice. "I was hoping we were finally rid of him."

"Problem?" Sabrina asked.

"Big problem," Zelda replied. "I still think he's trying to expose us as witches. I just wish I could find some concrete evidence."

"Well, it's nice to see some things haven't changed," Sabrina mumbled to herself.

"What was that?" Zelda asked.

"Nothing," Sabrina replied, realizing that she was not going to get any good information if she got stuck listening to this stranger talk about his recent trip back in time. "Should we leave them alone?"

"Definitely," Zelda said as she turned and led Sabrina back to the kitchen so that Hilda could have some time with her boyfriend. Sabrina wanted to ask what had happened with President Banning, but she figured now was not the time to bring up more unimportant facts. She needed to find out what was going on, and she suspected that she needed to do it quickly—time was always a factor in her spells gone wrong.

"That man is trouble," Zelda said as she began slamming cabinets open and shut, looking for something. "I just wish I could catch him in the act."

Sabrina really didn't have time for this con-versation, with the world the way it was, but she realized that something positive could come out of this mangled spell. Maybe they could prove once and for all whether Richard was trying to expose the Spellman family over two hundred years ago. At least then Hilda would be able to get some closure.

"Why do you think he's trying to expose us?" Sabrina asked as her aunt continued to bang around the kitchen, nearly taking a cabinet door off its hinges. "And what are you looking for?"

"Herbal tea," Zelda replied as she finally found it in the cabinet where it was always stored. She must have been really upset to have forgotten her very specific organization of the kitchen cabinets. She started to brew up some water in what Sabrina used to call "the mortal way," with an actual teapot on the stove.

Sabrina watched as her aunt nearly burned herself on the flames. "Aunt Zelda, calm down. You're going to hurt yourself," she said as she pulled her aunt over to sit at the table. Sabrina went back to the counter and took over making the tea for her aunt, getting out a cup and spoon.

"I'm sorry," Zelda said, trying to calm herself at the kitchen table. "He just gets me so mad."

"But why?" Sabrina asked again. "What has he been doing?"

"It's nothing specific," Zelda replied. "But every time he comes over, he seems to be trying to force Hilda to use magic in front of him. So far, she's managed to avoid the topic through the usual tricks of playing coy and the like. When that doesn't work, she uses some Black Market Magic. But she won't be able to fool him for long. Eventually he's going to realize that she doesn't have any powers."

"And then what?" Sabrina asked as the teapot whistled, indicating that the water had begun to boil.

"That's what I'm afraid of," Zelda replied.

The kitchen door swung open, and Hilda

came into the room, yelling back to Richard, "No, that's okay. I want to surprise you."

"What now?" Zelda asked.

"Oh, Richard asked me to whip up a special welcome home meal for him," Hilda replied, heading toward the refrigerator.

"When you say 'whip up' . . . ," Zelda started to say.

"Yes, he meant magic," Hilda replied. "Don't worry, I told him to wait in the living room while I zapped up a surprise."

Instead of going to the refrigerator, Sabrina was surprised to see that Hilda had opened the secret pantry in the wall beside it. She watched as her aunt pulled out a few packets of what looked to be some round seeds before making sure that the pantry door was fully closed. When it was shut, it conveniently looked just like another part of the wall. Back in Sabrina's reality, the secret pantry was where the family hid all their ingredients for magical spells.

"Why couldn't he zap it up himself?" Zelda asked.

"Now what kind of welcome home gift would that be?" Hilda gave by way of an answer as she took a seed from each packet and placed them on a serving platter she had pulled from a cupboard. She then grabbed the teapot from Sabrina's hands after the young witch had pour Zelda's tea.

Sabrina watched as her aunt carefully spilled out some of the boiling water onto the seeds, which immediately began to tremble on the serving dish. Out of the corner of her eye, Sabrina noticed that the kitchen door was creeping open, but before she could say anything, it swung wide.

"Hilda, is everything okay?" Richard asked as he came into the kitchen. "What's taking so long?"

When Sabrina's attention returned to the serving platter, she was surprised to find a fully cooked turkey with stuffing, potatoes, and even cranberry sauce resting on it.

"Now you've ruined the surprise," Hilda said, covering for her fake spell.

"A traditional thanksgiving dinner?" Richard asked.

"In honor of your return from the past," Hilda said. "And I was even going to zap myself into a traditional Puritan costume to serve it."

"I didn't go back that far in the past," he reminded her.

"But that was such an important time in mortal history," Hilda replied, as if overcompensating for the fact that she was hiding that she was a witch. "I thought you'd be pleased."

"Leave it to you to serve up the perfect welcome home meal," Richard said, smiling, as he took the platter from her so she wouldn't have to carry it into the dining room herself. "You could still whip up the costume, though."

"Nope, the surprise is ruined," she replied, following him.

Sabrina watched as they left the room, wondering how important Puritans and Thanksgiving were in this alternate universe. Back before things had gotten screwy, she'd never imagined that her aunt would be dressing up and serving Thanksgiving meals, since Puritans and witches didn't exactly have such a great history. Sabrina reasoned that her aunt must really like the guy. She had to admit that he seemed nice enough.

"See what I mean?" Zelda said as soon as the door was shut.

"Ummm . . . no?" Sabrina honestly replied.

"Why couldn't he whip up the meal?" Zelda asked. "And why did he sneak in while she was making it? And why did he still want her to zap up the costume?"

"I think you might be reading too much into it," Sabrina replied as she brought her aunt's tea over to her.

"Oops," Hilda said as she quickly returned to the kitchen. "Almost forgot the pumpkin pie."

"Hilda, this has got to stop," Zelda said as she followed her sister behind the kitchen counter.

"Well, you can't stop a dinner until you have

dessert," Hilda replied cutely as she tried to push past her sister to get into the pantry.

"It's not even lunchtime," Zelda reminded her sister.

"Don't be picky," Hilda said.

"He's just trying to trap you into using magic," Zelda persisted.

"No, he's not, Zellie," she replied. "But while you're so worried about him catching me, he *will* think something is up if I don't return with a pumpkin pie in a few seconds."

"Fine," Zelda said reluctantly as she opened the secret pantry for her sister.

"Hilda, I was thinking maybe cheesecake," Richard said as he came into the kitchen.

Sabrina immediately swung into action by grabbing Richard's arm and turning him toward her, hoping he hadn't noticed the open pantry. "So, Richard," she said, distracting him. "Tell me all about the seventeen hundreds."

"There's not much to tell," he started to say, but Sabrina hardly heard him. She was too busy looking over his shoulder as Zelda flung a little seed over to her sister and shut the pantry door. Sabrina did her best not to react when her aunt dropped the seed on the floor.

"Is everything okay?" Richard asked as he started to turn to Hilda.

"I don't know much about that century,"

Sabrina said, hoping her comment matched the last thing that he had said, since she hadn't even heard him.

"Really?" he asked. "You didn't know we won the Revolution? What are they teaching in schools these days?"

Whoops, she thought.

Luckily Richard continued speaking even though Sabrina was still focused on what was behind him. The only problem was that he had turned slightly, so now the secret pantry was just within his line of sight. Sabrina could tell that her aunt could not risk opening it for fear of being seen.

As Richard droned on, Sabrina watched Zelda join Hilda on the floor behind the counter and search for the seed. She tried to come up with a reason to get him out of the room, but nothing really came to mind except that his dinner would get cold. Unfortunately Sabrina was afraid that he would just say it could be magically reheated and then Hilda would have to fake yet another spell.

Finally she saw her aunts get up, but they didn't seem to have the seed in their hands. She also noticed that Zelda looked like she was a little angry. Wordlessly, Hilda had her sister step back as she took the teapot off the stove and poured the remaining water onto the floor.

A look of joy crossed Hilda's face as she bent back down behind the counter. "Here we are," she said, coming up from behind the counter with the newly made cheesecake.

Richard stopped in the middle of whatever he was saying to Sabrina to admire the freshly conjured cheesecake without noticing the slightly disheveled cook. "It looks wonderful," he said.

"Now let's eat," Hilda replied as she ushered him back into the dining room.

"See, nothing wrong there," Sabrina said, covering for the strange events that had just played themselves out. "Just another normal day in the Spellman home."

"Or for what passes as normal, at least," Zelda said as she took a sip of her tea and then a quick look at her watch. "Oh, no. I'm going to be late for class."

Zelda got up from her seat, leaving the practically full cup of tea behind. After giving her niece a peck on the cheek, she opened the secret pantry and took something out of it, but Sabrina couldn't see what it was. "You stay here and get some more rest," Zelda said as she clasped the mysterious item in her hand. "I'll talk to your other professors and see if you're missing anything today."

"I was hoping we could talk some more," Sabrina said. "I've got a bunch of questions."

"Oh, honey, I wish I could, but I have to get right back to campus. I have a lot of Black Market Magic to prepare before today's physics of magic lesson," Zelda said as she looked down into her hand. "I always have to stay a step ahead of my mortal students."

Sabrina tried to catch a glimpse of what her aunt was holding, but she wasn't quite able to make it out.

Before Sabrina could question her aunt about Black Market Magic, Zelda looked at whatever she was concealing in her hand, said, "Adams College," and disappeared.

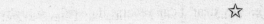

Chapter 8

Alone in the kitchen, Sabrina opened the secret pantry and saw a variety of tricks that she assumed were from the Black Magic Market that her aunts kept mentioning. Unfortunately, none of the items had labels on them. Sabrina figured that since these were not exactly legal products in this alternate universe, then it made sense not to advertise their contents. Unfortunately that was of no help to Sabrina, who needed all the magical help she could get to reverse her spell.

Sabrina closed the door to the secret pantry, looking at the painting of Aunt Louisa staring back at her. She was used to the blank stare from the portrait, because her aunt only spoke on rare occasions in her reality. Sabrina wondered if the portrait was still alive in this new altered state. "I don't suppose you can help me," Sabrina said to the painting.

"Yes, my dear, I can reverse the spell," a high-pitched voice responded. After a brief moment of excitement, Sabrina realized that it was not Aunt Louisa who had spoken.

"Salem, knock it off," Sabrina said, turning to find the cat giggling behind her.

"Well, what did you expect?" Salem asked. "The whole world turned upside down *except* for the talking picture in the kitchen?"

"As opposed to the talking cat at my feet?" Sabrina replied.

"Good point," he said. "So, what have we learned?"

"Absolutely nothing," Sabrina said. "Except there's some fake magic stored in the secret pantry now."

"I could have told you that," Salem said. "Some detective you are."

"You knew about the magic?" Sabrina asked.

"Hilda used it earlier to pop over to the coffee-house," he replied.

"That's great," Sabrina said as she picked him up off the floor and opened the pantry again. "Do you remember which of these things she used to zap her to the coffeehouse?"

"Of course," Salem said. "It was a gumball-size thing that smelled slightly like tuna."

"Are you sure?" she asked skeptically.

"Hey, I'm never wrong when I use food as my

basis of comparison," he replied as he stuck his face into the cabinet. "There. The little bag with the orange twist-tie over toward the side."

Sabrina picked up the bag he had indicated and gave it a sniff. She smelled nothing, and gave the cat a look of doubt.

"Never trust a human nose," he said as he stuck his head closer to the bag. "That's the one. But where are you going?"

"The only way to turn things back is with magic," Sabrina said. "I need to get to the Witches' Council."

"Have you been paying attention?" Salem asked. "What makes you think they'll have magic?"

"I'm out of other options," Sabrina said. "And even if they don't have magic, they probably have more information than we do right now."

Salem couldn't argue with that logic, considering they currently knew absolutely nothing.

Sabrina took one of the little balls out of the bag, still not smelling any tuna. Keeping Salem tucked into her right arm, she held the ball in her left hand. Taking a deep breath, she braced herself for whatever was about to happen. "Witches' Council," she said.

Nothing happened.

She looked at Salem, and he looked back at her. "Maybe we need to say it together?" he suggested.

Together they braced themselves and said, "Witches' Council."

This time, something did happen. Aunt Hilda came back through the door into the kitchen.

"More dessert," she said as she pushed past Sabrina and Salem to get to the pantry.

"No, thanks," Sabrina replied, which evoked a loud "meow" from an always hungry Salem.

"Not for you," Hilda said as she pulled something out of the pantry. "For Richard. He's changed his mind and would prefer the pumpkin pie."

"Then why didn't he just transform it into a pumpkin pie himself?" Sabrina asked.

"He says he loves my magical cooking," Hilda replied.

"Speaking of magic," Sabrina said, holding the little ball out to her aunt, "I can't get this thing to work."

Hilda continued to prepare dessert for Richard while she looked to see what was in her niece's hand. "Where did you want to go?"

"New York City," Sabrina replied, knowing that if she told her aunt about wanting to go to the Witches' Council it would raise all sorts of questions that she didn't want to answer. Since New York City was fairly close to Hoboken, she figured that was the easiest thing to say, even though they were technically in two different states.

"You know Molecular Transference Pellets don't have that kind of range," Hilda said as she spilled a drop of the still warm tea water on her seed. "You can only get twenty-five miles out of those things, tops."

"Are you sure you don't need any help?" Richard asked as he came into the kitchen.

"Here it is," Hilda said, holding up a newly created pumpkin pie. "I swear, you can't be away from me for a second."

Sabrina watched as Hilda and her boyfriend went back out to the dining room.

"Aunt Zelda may have a point," Sabrina said, still holding Salem and the Molecular Transference Pellet. "Richard does keep popping in whenever Aunt Hilda is pretending to do magic."

"So what are we going to do now?" Salem asked.

"Since we can't get to the Witches' Council using fake magic," Sabrina said, "we're going to need some real magic. I know my roommates are already using their powers, so I guess we should go home."

"Wouldn't you rather use the bus?" Salem asked, skeptical of the fake magic she held in her hand. "Or walk?"

"Not really," she replied, not trusting that magic bus she had already been on today, or what the streets of Westbridge had in store for them. Sabrina closed her palm on the pellet and said, "My house."

Sabrina and Salem felt a jolt as they were flung to the off-campus house she shared with her friends. The spell was noticeably different from the real magic that Sabrina had been used to since she'd turned sixteen. Instead of being instantaneously transferred to her desired destination, Sabrina actually felt the time pass as the seconds ticked away while she and Salem seemed to be in some weird, dark tunnel. Finally, the darkness began to recede, and the pair found themselves in the middle of Sabrina's living room.

"Roxie? Miles? Morgan?" Sabrina yelled, but got no response. "Is anyone here?"

"Great," Salem said. "Now we're stuck here with no magic."

"There's got to be something somewhere," Sabrina said, putting Salem down. "Let's try my room."

Together they went into the room that Sabrina shared with Roxie. Knowing they wouldn't find anything in Sabrina's stuff, they started on her roommate's side of the room. Sabrina busied herself by looking through the dresser drawers while Salem searched around the desk.

"I can't believe it," Sabrina said as she dug deep into a drawer.

"Find something?" Salem asked.

"A pink sweater," Sabrina said, pulling the item from the dresser. "I didn't think Roxie owned anything pink."

"Can we stay on the subject?" Salem asked. "I think I've got something that could be useful."

"What is it?" Sabrina asked, putting the sweater back and heading for the desk.

"It looks like somebody has a Magic CD-ROM," Salem said, holding the disk up with his paw.

"Woo-hoo!" Sabrina cheered as she took the CD from Salem and placed it into Roxie's computer. "I'd ask you to watch the door, Salem, but we both know you're the worst lookout in history."

"I was born to rule the world," Salem replied smugly, "not guard the doors."

As soon as the CD booted up, Sabrina began to search its contents for the spell that had gotten her into all this trouble. It took her a moment to get used to the program since it was slightly different from the one she'd owned pre-magical mix-up.

"Great," Sabrina said, sounding anything *but* happy. "The See-Things-Through-My-Eyes spell isn't here, for some reason."

"Did you really think you'd be able to solve this without learning a valuable life lesson first?" Salem asked.

"Silly me," Sabrina replied. "I guess the rules for magic are just as crazy now as they were before. At least we can look up how to do a real Molecular Transference spell."

"Good, because I got a little seasick in that crazy tunnel we took over here," Salem said. "Of course, if I had been given some food before we'd left, my stomach would have probably been more settled."

"That is some crazy logic you have there," Sabrina replied.

"Hey, I use whatever works," he answered back.

"'Molecular Transference Spell,'" Sabrina read as she pulled up the proper spell. "'Just point your finger and think of where you want to go.'"

"Well, that was no help whatsoever," Salem said.

"No, wait," Sabrina said as she read on. "It gives a tip on how to do the spell if you're suffering a finger malfunction."

"What about a brain malfunction?" Salem said.

"You're not being a big help here, cat," Sabrina said as she read on. "All I have to do is press the escape key on the computer."

"How appropriate," he said, noting the aptly used pun.

"Do you think it's safe?" she asked, a bit uncomfortable with the idea of using magic in this strange reality they were stuck in.

"Safer than doing nothing," Salem said. "Besides, it's almost time for lunch, and I'm not planning on another dry meat by-product meal that comes in a pouch and is made especially for the friendly family feline."

"Hold on, Salem," she said as she took the cat into her arms again.

Sabrina placed her finger over the escape key and thought of the Witches' Council in Hoboken, New Jersey. Holding tightly to Salem, she braced for whatever was about to come, and pushed down on the key.

Suddenly Sabrina got dizzy as the room began to spin. She could hardly hear Salem as he called her name while the world got all blurry. Immediately Sabrina could tell that this was a whole different kind of blurry than she usually saw when looking into a flashback. As Sabrina fell to the floor, she had one last though before going unconscious: *This can't be right.*

Chapter 9

☆

☆

"Wh-Where am I?" Sabrina asked groggily as she awoke in what appeared to be a hospital room.

"It's okay, Sabrina," Zelda said, taking her niece's hand. "We're here."

"You're in the hospital," Hilda added. "And you're going to be fine."

"What happened?" Sabrina asked as the room and her aunts started to come into focus.

"As best we can tell," Zelda said, "you tried to use Roxie's Magic CD-ROM."

"Oh, yeah, I had to get . . ." But Sabrina caught herself before she mentioned the Witches' Council. She still didn't want to give her aunts more questions. She figured things had already gotten bad enough.

"Get what?" Hilda asked.

"Something," she replied.

"But you know witches can't use real magic,"

Zelda said. "It was too powerful and knocked you out. Luckily Harvey found you and got in touch with us."

"Harvey?" Sabrina asked, looking around the room but not seeing him there.

"He'll be back in a bit," Hilda said. "The doctors don't like to have mortals hanging around. It makes them nervous."

Feeling her strength returning, Sabrina sat up in her bed. "But I thought that witches were the ones who had to be careful. Where are we?"

"A private hospital for witches," Zelda replied.

"So then Harvey still knows I'm a witch?" Sabrina asked.

Once again her aunts gave each other looks of concern. Sabrina nearly giggled because this was like the tenth time she had seen them do this today alone. Of course, she didn't giggle, because laughter was rather inappropriate at the moment.

"Sabrina, we're a little worried," Zelda said. "All this forgetting you've had today . . ."

"And trying to use magic," Hilda added.

"It's not healthy," Zelda said. "We spoke to your father, and he agreed that we should have you talk to a professional."

"What kind of professional?" Sabrina asked, although she suspected that she knew what her aunts were talking about.

"He specializes in witches who have a hard time dealing with the fact they are half-mortal and have lost their powers," Hilda replied.

"We always knew we should have had you talk with him when you were sixteen," Zelda said. "But when your father sent you to us, we thought we could help you through the transition ourselves. I guess we were wrong."

Sabrina's mind was racing. She knew if she was going to have to seek professional help that her aunts would never let her out of their sight and she wouldn't be able to get to the Witches' Council. Even though Sabrina still had no idea what the Council could do, it was her only plan. And right now, things didn't look good.

"I'm sure I'll be fine," she said. "Just a little more rest."

"That's what we thought this morning," Zelda said.

"Morning?" Sabrina asked. "How long have I been unconscious?"

"A few hours now," Zelda said. "We don't know how long you were out before Harvey found you. It's three o'clock now."

"I need to get to the newspaper office," Sabrina said as she started to get up, but her aunts gently held her back down.

"We've already called Josh to let him know

you're not feeling well," Zelda said. "He put us in touch with your boss, Mike, so we could let him know you'd be in when you're better."

"And he was okay?" Sabrina asked.

"Perfectly fine," Zelda said.

"Although some annoying woman did get on the phone and start yelling," Hilda jumped in to add. "She seemed a little intense."

Sabrina easily reasoned that it must have been Christy who had grabbed the phone. She wasn't quite sure if they were still working on the supplement together, but she assumed that if her absence from work was going to send the reporter into hysterics, things would be difficult for Sabrina once she got everything back to normal.

"Now forget about work," Hilda said. "We need to focus on your problem."

"But I'm fine," Sabrina pleaded with her aunts to believe her obvious lie.

"No, you're not," Zelda insisted. "In fact, things have gotten worse, what with you trying to use magic. No, the best thing to do is to speak to a professional."

"But . . . ," Sabrina started, then realized that she couldn't come up with something else to say. Luckily she didn't have to.

"There you are," Richard said as he popped into the room.

"Okay, this is starting to get annoying," Sabrina mumbled softly to Zelda, hoping that her other aunt didn't here.

"Richard, how did you find me?" Hilda asked as she got up to shut the hospital room door for fear of a doctor stumbling in and blowing their cover in front of the mortal.

"Simple locator spell," he said, peering out the door as Hilda shut it. "Where are we?"

"It's a private hospital," Zelda said. "Sabrina's suffering from a little magical malady."

"Are you okay?" he asked Sabrina with a definite note of concern in his voice.

"She's fine," Hilda said, trying to divert his attention from her niece before they had to explain too much about her condition. "But the doctors really don't want her to have too many visitors right now."

"I completely understand," he said. "Meet me later?"

"Of course," Hilda said, giving him a kiss.

Sabrina and Zelda turned away from the public display of affection out of respect and a little bit of discomfort.

"Feel better, Sabrina," Richard said as he disappeared.

"Don't say it," Hilda said to her sister.

"I'm really more concerned about Sabrina right now," Zelda said. "I don't have time to get into a discussion about your poor choice in men."

"And yet somehow you still manage to make a comment," Hilda said, catching on to her sister's implied insult.

"Knock, knock," Harvey said as he tapped on the door.

"Come in, Harvey," Zelda said as she and her sister stood while Sabrina stayed in bed, making sure her hospital gown was not bunching in the wrong places.

"I found your cat wandering around outside," Harvey said, handing him to Sabrina.

"Salem has been acting weird all day," Hilda said as she moved to take the cat from her niece.

"That's okay," Sabrina said as she held tightly to the cat. "He probably just senses that something's wrong with me."

"How are you feeling?" Harvey asked.

"Better," Sabrina replied.

"We'll let you two have some time alone," Zelda said as she ushered her sister out of the room.

"I hear you saved me," Sabrina said.

"Well, I just popped over to see Morgan, and your cat was acting all crazy," Harvey said as he gave Salem a little rub behind the ears. "He led me to you."

"Aren't you just the little hero," Sabrina said giving Salem a tight squeeze of gratitude.

"You're aunts said that you've been having some . . . difficulties?" Harvey said tentatively.

Sabrina immediately realized that she finally had someone with magic who could help her. The question was whether Harvey would believe her crazy story, since her aunts already hadn't. Then again in the past she had always counted on Harvey to believe her even when she'd had to make up ridiculous excuses for things. After a momentary twinge of regret for lying to him so much when they had been in high school, Sabrina decided that he would have to trust her now.

"Look, Harvey, I need to tell you something, and I'm not sure you're going to believe me," Sabrina said, motioning for him to sit in the chair beside her.

"Of course I'll believe you," he said. "You haven't lied to me since high school. At least, that I know of."

Okay, Sabrina thought, *I guess I deserved that one.*

"I cast a spell and now the world has turned upside down," Sabrina said. "In reality witches are supposed to have magic and mortals are powerless."

There was a long pause from Harvey that Sabrina was already getting used to receiving from her aunts. She knew that he wasn't buying it.

"Your aunts said—" he started.

"That I'm having some kind of delayed denial and can't accept that I lost my powers," Sabrina finished his sentence for him. "I know that's what they think, but it's not true. I *did* have magic just yesterday. I used it to cast a spell so my friends would understand what it's like to be me. I guess it worked a little too well."

"So you're saying your spell changed the entire world?" Harvey asked.

"Yes," Sabrina said, feeling ever so guilty since he chose to phrase it that way.

"Sabrina, magic just doesn't backfire that badly," Harvey said.

"Well, there's one good thing for this alternate reality," Salem chimed in.

"Did your cat just talk?" Harvey asked, jumping out of his seat.

Sabrina realized that, just like her aunts, Harvey had expected Salem to be a normal cat. This could work to her benefit. "Yes, he did," Sabrina said. "Let me guess: Before today, you probably thought he was just a normal cat."

"Yeah," he said in shock.

"I'm still having some trouble figuring out the rules of this place," Salem said as Harvey looked on in surprise. Apparently it was normal for animals to speak—it just was not normal for this particular feline to speak.

"Just out of curiosity," Sabrina began a question

that she knew she shouldn't ask, "what happened when you found out I was a witch?"

"Let's try to stay on topic here," Salem interrupted before Harvey could answer. "Look, Harv, I know this seems weird, but honestly, in your whole history with Sabrina, when haven't things been a little weird?"

"The cat has a point," Harvey said.

"How did you know that was still true?" Sabrina asked Salem.

"I took a shot," he replied.

"Harvey, I know this doesn't make any sense," Sabrina said. "But I'm telling you the truth. And I have to make things right before the world goes insane."

"Too late," Salem said.

"What?" she said.

"Tell you later," he replied as he directed their attention back to Harvey.

"What do you need me to do?" Harvey finally asked.

Sabrina and Salem shared in a sigh of relief.

"Can you zap me to Hoboken?" Sabrina asked. "I need to see some people, who I hope can set things right."

"But I can't use my magic on you anymore," Harvey said. "Mortals can only use so many spells on a witch. Beyond that, the magic becomes ineffective."

Once again, the crazy rules worked against Sabrina. The same thing had happened to her and Harvey long before she had cast this spell that had gone majorly wrong. That was how he had found out she was a witch. Back in high school, she had used so much magic on him that he had grown immune to it.

"I doubt this will work," Sabrina said, although trying her best to remain positive. "But Harvey, do you think you could try to do an undo spell on my spell?"

"It's worth a try," he replied, stepping back to give himself some room for magic.

"Well, let's go," Salem said impatiently.

Sabrina clamped her hand over the cat's mouth.

"Sabrina's spell went very wrong,
Set life back to how we belong,"

Harvey chanted, and gave a little point of his finger.

Sabrina couldn't help but get a little charge out of watching him cast a spell since that kind of thing usually happened the other way around, with her working the magic. It was kind of weird for her to see things through his eyes for a change. Suddenly Sabrina began to feel the stirrings of a life lesson coming on.

"Did it work?" Salem asked.

"Let's see," Sabrina said as she pointed to her hospital gown, intending to change into her street clothes. Nothing happened.

Then Harvey gave a little point and a bouquet of flowers appeared in a vase beside Sabrina.

"So now what do we do?" Salem asked in a tone that indicated he was about to give up.

"I have to get to Hoboken," Sabrina said.

"What about my magic vacuum?" Harvey asked. "Do you think you could fly it?"

"I don't see why not," Sabrina said, excited to finally have a plan. "I'm a pro on mine. Well, except for that one ticket."

"And that nice crash landing in Los Angeles," Salem oh-so-helpfully added.

"I'll have to pop home and get it," Harvey said. "I was doing some repairs, so I'll have to finish up first. Should I meet you back here?"

"Too risky," Sabrina said. "My aunts won't let me leave. I'll have to sneak out."

"Why don't we meet at the coffeehouse?" Harvey suggested.

"Good idea," Sabrina replied. "I'll meet you out back in case Aunt Hilda shows up. Get there as soon as you can."

"See you soon," Harvey said, then zapped himself out of the hospital room.

"Now what's this about the world going

crazy?" she asked Salem as soon as Harvey was gone.

"While you were out," Salem said. "I had a chance to look around."

"Give me the highlights," Sabrina said, worried about her aunts coming back to the room.

"Well, the moon is a lot closer than it used to be," Salem said.

"How close?" Sabrina asked.

"Vermont," the cat replied. "And that's not all. The world is going haywire. Sabrina, mortals are using magic to do everything. I'm afraid that pretty soon Earth is going to become just like the Other Realm."

"Then we may never find Hoboken," Sabrina finished the thought for Salem.

"Exactly," the cat agreed.

"I need to get changed," Sabrina said as she sprang from the bed. Sabrina was feeling much better. The effects of her reaction to the spell she had cast on Roxie's computer were apparently gone. "Salem, start thinking of a way to distract my aunts. We're getting out of here."

Sabrina picked up her clothes, which were hanging neatly in the closet. Once dressed, she figured she could just hop out the window and make a break for it since her room was on the ground floor. Unfortunately, before she reached the bathroom, the door to her room slowly opened, a strange man knocking on it came in.

Sabrina stopped in her tracks.

"Miss Spellman?" the man said as he came through the door. "I'm Dr. Young. Your aunts thought we should have a little talk."

Chapter 10

☆

☆

"Are you going somewhere, Miss Spellman?" Dr. Young asked.

Sabrina froze with her clothes in her arms, mere steps away from the bathroom. Slowly she turned to face the doctor, who she assumed was the therapist her aunts had spoken of earlier. "I was cold," she said, thinking quickly. "These thin hospital gowns don't really keep in the heat."

"We could adjust the thermostat," Dr. Young said as he moved toward the mechanism.

"No, that's okay," Sabrina said, picking Salem up. "I'll just be a second."

"And you're bringing your cat?" the doctor asked, with an eyebrow raised.

"He doesn't like strangers," Sabrina said as she continued into the bathroom.

Sabrina closed the door before the doctor could ask any more questions. She knew that he knew the only reason for her to put on her clothes was that she planned to leave. Now she had to change clothes, convince the doctor she was staying put, and then find a way to get rid of him so she could sneak away.

She surveyed the bathroom, looking for an escape. Unfortunately, the one window was way too small for her to climb out of. However, her pint-size partner could fit through it easily.

"Now what?" Salem asked.

"I have to get rid of that therapist," Sabrina said.

"Let's hear it for stating the obvious," Salem replied. "How?"

"One thing at a time," Sabrina replied as she opened the small window. "I need you to get to the coffeehouse and tell Harvey I've been delayed."

"Are you sure you don't want me to stay here?" Salem asked as she placed him on the windowsill. "You're not exactly the best liar. You might need some help."

"Somehow I think if I keep whispering to my cat, the therapist will find it hard to believe that I'm sane," Sabrina said.

"Good point," Salem said as he scurried out the window.

After watching him leave, Sabrina shut the window and turned back into the room, picking up her clothes.

"Think, Sabrina. Think," she whispered to herself as she slowly changed. "The only way to get him out of here is to convince him I'm okay about not having my powers. Which would be ever so much easier if I had any memory of life without powers."

Sabrina thought about her little conundrum as she finished dressing. Unfortunately no easy solution came. She waited as long as she could in the bathroom, but figured if she stayed in there any longer, Dr. Young would send her aunts in to check on her.

As she stepped out of the bathroom, Sabrina immediately noticed that the therapist had set up a conversation area by pulling the two guest chairs over so that they faced each other. He had already made himself comfortable in the chair blocking the only door leading out of the room. Still trying to figure out what she was going to say, Sabrina took the chair that he offered her.

"Would you like to talk about why you're here?" Dr. Young asked as he took out his pen and starting making some notes on a pad of paper.

"I guess you just dive right into things, don't you?" Sabrina replied, stalling for time.

"I like to get to the heart of the matter," he answered. "But do you prefer to talk about something else?"

"No, no, that's fine," Sabrina said. "I was

doing some work on my roommate's computer and I accidentally hit a key that activated a spell."

"So it was an accident?" the doctor asked.

Sabrina had heard jokes about how therapists only repeated what their patients said and turned it into a question. She nearly laughed over the fact that she was getting to experience it first-hand. Then again, she figured spontaneous laughter would be another thing Dr. Young would question, so she held it in.

"Oh, yeah, purely an accident," Sabrina said. "I know my aunts probably told you that for some reason I've been having some really delayed emotions about losing my powers when I was sixteen."

"Yes, why do you think these feelings have manifested themselves now?" he asked.

Sabrina was impressed by how he could take her phrase and turn it into such a formal question. Again she nearly giggled when she realized that he had just asked her the same exact thing she had said. "Beats me," she replied.

Sabrina couldn't help but think that Salem was right about the fact that she was a lousy liar. Oh sure, she had told many cover stories to explain her magic to her friends in the past, but they were usually quite far-fetched, and she was lucky that her uncommonly gullible friends had believed them. Somehow, she didn't think the old "it was all a dream" excuse would work on the good doctor.

"Has your life been especially difficult lately?" Dr. Young asked, still writing notes on his pad.

Sabrina couldn't figure out what he could be writing, since she had hardly said anything. Then again, he probably had to pretend he was making progress if he expected to get paid. "Not really," she answered. "In fact, things have been pretty great."

"Better than usual?" he asked.

"Much better," she replied, thinking back to before she had cast the stupid spell. Since it had been such a crazy day, Sabrina had forgotten all about the scholarship, the science journal, and her *almost* shared byline on the paper. She regretted the fact that, rather than enjoying her good fortune, she was stuck in this wild world of a spell gone wrong.

"If things are so good," the doctor continued pressing her, "why do you think you cast the spell?"

For a moment she thought he was talking about the See-Things-Through-My-Eyes spell, but he had really meant the one that had knocked her out and sent her to the hospital. "I said it was an accident," Sabrina replied.

"But we both know it wasn't," he gently shot back to her.

"No, it wasn't." Sabrina agreed, figuring that the only way to get the doctor out of the room was by giving him the answers he wanted. So she decided to tell him a slightly skewed version of the truth that had gotten her into the mess in the first place. "Things had been great. Much better than normal. But none of my friends seemed to be happy for me."

"Why do you think your friends weren't happy for you?" he asked.

She wondered how much this guy got paid to turn everything she said into a question. "Well, they were happy," she replied. "But they weren't really celebrating with me."

"Do you need a celebration every time you do something big?" he asked.

"No," she quickly replied. "But I just wish they would realize how hard it is for me to do things, because I'm so different."

"Because you don't have magic powers?" he asked.

For a moment Sabrina had been so into her story that she had forgotten that in this reality, that was what made her different from her roommates. She plunged ahead with her story, anyway. "Right," she said. "They don't know how hard it is to live with that secret."

"And since they have magic, their lives are much easier?" the doctor asked.

"No," Sabrina said. "It's not about the magic. It's about having to keep this secret. If they knew how well I'm doing and still keeping this secret, they'd be even happier for me."

The doctor let that statement hang in the air for a moment.

"Well, that sounded a little egotistical," Sabrina said, making her own realization without the professional's help.

"And is that why you cast the spell?" Dr. Young asked. "Because you wanted your friends to be even more impressed by what you can do?"

"I guess it was," Sabrina realized. "Do you think I'm insecure?"

"Do you?"

"That repeating thing you do is starting to get annoying," she said. "But I guess I do have this need to achieve and make sure everyone knows how I'm doing."

"And how do you think that makes your friends feel?" he asked.

"I guess I never really thought about that," Sabrina replied.

"Then I guess we made a bit of a break-through," the doctor replied as he stood up.

"Are you going?" Sabrina asked, momentarily forgetting that his departure was her ultimate objective here.

"Just for now," he replied. "I'm sorry, but things

have been a little hectic since the Moon landed on Earth. Even though it's back in place now, I've got patients lined up around the block."

"That's okay," Sabrina replied, getting back to her original plan. "You should go. I know how people drive when there's a full moon in its normal spot in the universe. I can't imagine how it affects them when it's right next door."

"We can certainly set up an appointment for later," the doctor added.

"Yes, fine," she replied, practically pushing him out the door. "Talk to my aunts about it."

As soon as the door was shut, Sabrina headed for the window. She was thrilled over the fact that not only had the therapist helped her out, but he had done so in such a short time that she might even beat Harvey to the coffeehouse.

More importantly Sabrina realized that she had learned a life lesson: She shouldn't feel the need to get praise whenever something good happened to her. She should also stop bragging so much to her friends about it, since her life was pretty perfect, even though she had to hide her magic.

Sabrina had a feeling from past experience that once she acknowledged that she'd learned her lesson, the Witches' Council would fix the spell and everything would return to normal.

Chapter 11

As soon as Sabrina was out the window, she heard her aunts' voices in the room behind her.

"Sabrina, honey, we have to talk to you," Zelda said.

"It's about why you're here," Hilda added.

Before Sabrina heard anything more, she made a dash for it, knowing it wouldn't take long for her aunts to realize that she wasn't in the small room. Since the window was the only way out, it wasn't like they were going to search the hospital before they peeked outside. And she knew if they saw her, she would never get to the Witches' Council, and then, life lesson or not, she would never get things back to normal.

Before she was half a block away, Sabrina heard something that stopped her cold. Alarms were blaring. Afraid to look, she slowly turned back to the hospital and saw red lights flashing as the siren blared. "That's not a very secret hospital," Sabrina said to herself.

When she saw a team of hospital workers come out the front door, she jumped behind the nearest group of bushes. Looking between the leaves, she saw her aunts coming out as well. She couldn't hear anything from her place behind the bushes, but she could see her aunts conferring with the hospital staff. Sabrina didn't have to wonder what they had been talking about. After a few seconds, she watched as they scattered in different directions.

"This seems like overkill just for little ol' me," she said as she stepped out of her place behind the bushes once the coast was clear.

Sabrina pointed herself in the direction of the coffeehouse and started moving. Luckily she knew the neighborhood she was in and that she was within walking distance of her destination. She only hoped the streets hadn't changed that much, considering what Salem had told her about the world having gone a little crazy now that mortals had magic.

Staying close to the buildings, Sabrina negotiated her way through the Boston neighborhoods. Luckily most of her search party was dressed in white hospital uniforms so they'd be easy enough to spot. Whenever she saw a group of people walking by, she first confirmed that neither her aunts nor the hospital staff were among them, then got as close as possible to look like she was part of the group. Considering the hospital workers didn't know her that well, she assumed this would throw them off, since they were looking for someone traveling alone. There was, unfortunately, no way she was going to fool her aunts.

Mere blocks away from the coffeehouse, Sabrina had joined a pack of college students who looked like they were heading home from their afternoon classes. She didn't know any of the students, but was thankful that she could blend among them so easily—especially when she saw a pair of men dressed in white at the end of the street.

As Sabrina considered her options, she glanced back and saw that her aunts were only a few yards behind her. Luckily they were heading across the street and not looking in her direction. Sabrina gave a sigh of relief, glad for the small amount of luck she seemed to be having. And right about then, the group of students decided they were tired of walking and wanted to fly home on their vacuums!

As one, the students lifted off the ground, leaving Sabrina totally alone and exposed. She dashed into the nearest alleyway, hoping the hospital workers and her aunts didn't see her. However her hopes were soon dashed when she heard quickened footsteps heading in her direction.

Sabrina looked back into the alley and did not like what she saw. Shadows filled the block-long stretch between buildings loaded with garbage bins and assorted large objects to hide behind. Although she was glad to see there were plenty of options for keeping hidden, she did not like the idea of heading into a darkened alleyway where anyone could jump out at her. Sabrina wished she still had her magic.

Sabrina took a tentative step down the alley as she heard her followers moving closer. Knowing she didn't have any time for caution, she ran behind the nearest garbage bin and dove toward the wall. Obviously Sabrina was a little too forceful, because she wound up flinging herself right through the brick wall.

Sabrina landed inside the darkened building on a cold stone floor. As she tried to orient herself to the fact that she had just fallen *through* a wall, she picked herself up off the ground. Once she got to her feet, a blast of light hit her as the room became illuminated. She turned back and saw a glass door behind her. Looking out, she could see into the alley, though she was sure that the door did not exist on the outside of the building.

"Welcome, welcome, little lady," a rather large and quite jovial man said to her as he approached.

"Welcome to Merlin's Make-believe Magic."

"Where?" she asked as the man took her hand and pulled her farther into the room that she now noticed was full of tables and displays with all sorts of magic-looking items of various sizes and shapes.

"Merlin's Make-believe Magic," he repeated. "Where witches go to get the latest in mostly magical items."

Sabrina surveyed the room, noticing jars of dust and bags of seeds, as well as a slew of weird objects—she couldn't imagine what *they* were. Considering the mostly magical items, and the salesmanlike quality of the happy fellow showing her around, Sabrina immediately knew where she was. "The Black Magic Market," she said, slightly above a whisper.

"Now, now, little lady," the happy man said. "We try to refrain from using that name around here. Merlin's is stocked with only the best products for the witch in need."

"How did you know I'm a witch?" she asked.

"The door is enchanted by a Mortals-Keep-Out spell," he said, indicating the porthole she had fallen through. "It allows witches to enter but keeps those pesky mortals out. You, too, can have one for your home—it's just $19.95. On sale today only."

"No, thanks," Sabrina replied, about to make a polite excuse and exit until she had a wonderful thought. "But do you have any Molecular Transference Pellets?"

"Ah, we're out of those at the moment," he said, looking quite depressed about it. "We always run out around vacation time, since witches are always looking for cheaper ways to get away from it all. Speaking of which, can I interest you in Virtual Sunglasses? They're the next best thing to actually being wherever you want to be."

"No," Sabrina replied, putting down the sunglasses that he had pointed into her hands, "though I actually do need to be somewhere. Hilda's coffeehouse. It's about three blocks from here."

"I realize it's hard being a witch in a mortal world," the salesman said. "But you can walk, can't you?"

"I should have been more specific," Sabrina replied. "I need to get there, but I need to do it unnoticed. Do you have any invisibility items?"

"Like a cape?" he asked.

"Exactly!" Sabrina replied, excitedly looking around the room.

"Nope," he replied. "But I do have a Transparency Smock somewhere. Only problem is, I can't find it."

"Because it's transparent?" Sabrina asked, knowing the answer.

"You catch on quick," he replied as he led her over to a long rack of various coats and other clothing. "I'm sure I have something around that can be helpful. Tell me, are bloodhounds on your trail?"

"No," Sabrina replied. "Just a group of witches."

"Oh, that will be easy," he said moving over to a table with rows of small, colorful cardboard boxes. "Are you a cat person or a dog person?"

"Well, I do have a cat," Sabrina replied. "So I guess I'd have to say that he's made me more of a dog lover."

"Can't say I blame you," the salesman replied, although Sabrina figured he would have been understanding no matter what animal she chose. "Take one of these animal crackers and you'll be turned into a dog for five minutes."

Sabrina watched as he placed the little cracker treat in her hand. It was in the shape of a Chihuahua.

"You don't have a golden retriever, by any chance?" she asked.

"I'm getting a shipment in next week," he replied.

Sabrina couldn't help but wonder how the man stayed in business considering he seemed to be out of half his stock. Then again, as she surveyed the makeshift room, she figured he wasn't spending a lot of money on a prime location. "How much?" she asked, expecting an expensive price.

"A quarter," he replied, sounding more than a little sad over the fact that he wasn't going to make much of a profit off her.

"That's it?" Sabrina asked as she dug into her pocket for the cash.

"They're out of season," he replied. "Around the time of the Westminster Dog Show I can get a good ten bucks a cracker. The walls are lined with boxes of the different breeds when all the witches head down to New York to compete."

Oddly enough Sabrina was pleased to know that witches in this reality were just as strange as the witches in her regular life. She exchanged the quarter for the Chihuahua animal cracker and thanked the salesman for his service.

"Are you sure I can't interest you in anything else?" he asked.

"I'm fine, thanks," she replied as she saw another customer coming through the secret door.

"It was a pleasure meeting you," the salesman said as he started heading over to the new arrival. "Please tell your witch friends about us."

"Oh, I certainly will," she replied after he had already moved away.

Sabrina took the cookie in her hand and glanced out the door into the alley. Noticing the coast was clear, she pushed her way through. Once outside again, she turned to find that there was only a brick wall behind her.

Sabrina bit into the cookie and felt absolutely nothing. Throwing caution to the wind, she swallowed the rest of the little snack, wishing she had some milk to go along with it. Although she knew there was plenty of milk at the coffee-house, she didn't really think that going inside was the best thing to do if she didn't want to get caught. Besides, she still had to get there first.

Seconds later Sabrina could feel the power of the animal cracker begin to take effect. It started with an overwhelming need for her to stick out her tongue and pant. She started feeling some-what excited—or at the very least, excitable—as was to be expected being a Chihuahua, she guessed. Then she began to shrink.

Sabrina was now looking at the world from a perspective of only a few inches off the ground. She looked down at her hands and found tiny little paws in their place. When she turned her head, she could see the back end of her body had been dogified as well. She checked around for a mirror or some kind of reflective device, but couldn't find anything to reveal her new look. Sabrina gave up the search for a mirror and figured she didn't have any time to waste.

Peeking out from the alley she noticed that the coast was clear. Stepping out she immediately noticed she could see herself in the window of the building she was next to, and took a moment to admire her new look. Impressed she tried to say "I look good," but all that came out was, "Yip!"

"Yip! Yip! Yip!" she said to the reflection in the window as she thought, *Great, I should have asked for a spell to make me a* talking *dog*.

Since going back to the sales guy was pointless, Sabrina scampered off to the coffeehouse. Thrilled by the speed at which she could move on four legs, Sabrina enjoyed her run, even though it felt like she had to go farther because she was so small.

As she approached the coffeehouse, Sabrina slowed to a walk and scoured the area to make sure her aunts weren't around. Since Hilda did own the place, the odds were good that she would be around or assume that her niece may be heading there. Even though nothing could be done now, Sabrina wished she and Harvey had agreed on a less obvious meeting place.

Looking in the window, Sabrina saw no sign of her aunt. She did, however, see Morgan, now dressed in a black silk ensemble, cleaning off a table. She was always amazed watching her roommate work, since it was so incredibly against Morgan's nature to do any "menial task." Of course, in this reality, things were considerably easier for Morgan. Sabrina watched as her roommate simply pointed her finger at the dirty mugs and plates to clean them. Sabrina wished she could do that in her normal day—things would be so much easier.

Immediately, Sabrina took back her last thought. That regret was what had gotten her into this in the first place. And now she realized she should just appreciate her gift for what it was. In her heart Sabrina knew that the Witches' Council would be able to help her.

"Oh, what a cute little doggie," she could hear Morgan say through the glass window.

Thanks, Sabrina thought, but only said, "Yip!"

Moving away from the window, Sabrina headed for the alley behind the coffeehouse to meet Harvey and Salem. As she went around, she couldn't help but think she was spending too much time in alleys today; however, this one was much more familiar and, for that fact alone, was safer.

"What do we have here?" Salem asked from his perch on top of a trash can. "A dog the size of a mouse? Looks like I'm going to have some fun."

And all Sabrina could say was, "Yip!"

Chapter 12

☆

"Well, little mouse-dog," Salem said with his back arched, looking ready to pounce. "We can do this the easy way or the hard way."

"Yip!" Sabrina said, both frightened and angry over the fact that Salem was mean enough to pick on a defenseless tiny dog. If only the salesman hadn't been out of golden retriever animal crackers. She was sure Salem wouldn't have had the nerve to pick on a dog that was bigger than he was.

"What's that you say?" Salem asked, playing cat and mouse-dog. "The hard way? If you insist."

Without warning, Salem pounced.

Sabrina dashed out from under the cat as he landed, headfirst, on the ground. He wasn't exactly the most graceful feline. Righting himself Salem lunged at Sabrina as she literally ran circles around him to make him dizzy. Luck continued to be on her side—or at least Salem's own gluttony was—since his penchant for eating made him somewhat slower. Sabrina's tiny size as a Chihuahua enabled her to keep moving, so that she managed to stay out of his grasp, hoping that the spell would wear off soon.

As Salem stalked her, slightly dizzy from the circling, Sabrina debated running away until she turned back into a human. The problem, however, was that she was afraid Salem would follow her and then no one would be there when Harvey finally showed up. She was thinking over her options when she realized that she had run herself into a corner.

"Now where are you going to go?" Salem asked as he slowly moved toward her.

"Yip!" she said, realizing she was out of options.

Just then Sabrina could feel the change coming over her. Salem must have noticed something going on as well, because he had the strangest look of shock on his face. Moments later Sabrina was back to her normal height dressed as she had been before the dogification.

"Sabrina?" Salem jumped back in surprise. "What were you doing as a dog?"

"Better question: What were you going to do to that poor little dog?" she replied.

"I was just having some fun," he said. "It's not

easy being stuck in this body. I have to take fun wherever I can get it, and sometimes playing with little doggies helps me through the day."

"That wasn't exactly playing, Salem," Sabrina scolded, not buying his poor pathetic cat act. "Where's Harvey?"

"I'm right here," Harvey said as he suddenly appeared on his flying vacuum cleaner.

Sabrina couldn't help but notice the cute little pink basket tied to the handle that really didn't match the rest of the machine.

"Nice accessory," she said, referring to the basket.

"It's from my little sister's toy vacuum," he replied. "I thought you could use it to hold Salem in."

Sabrina was impressed by his ingenuity.

"And it's just my color," Salem added sarcastically.

"Do you know how to ride one of these things?" Harvey asked.

"I used to all the time before things went haywire," Sabrina replied.

"But that was when you had your powers," Salem reminded her while checking out the stability of what was to be his seat for the ride. "Will you be able to stay on this thing without magic? And, more importantly, will you be able to keep me safely in this thing without magic?"

"That's a good point," Sabrina said, remembering back to her crazy bus ride earlier that day. "Maybe I should test it out first while you're still here, Harvey."

"Would you like me to come with you?" Harvey asked.

"I don't think the basket's big enough," Salem replied.

"It's okay," Sabrina said. "I don't think bringing a mortal with me to the Witches' Council is a good idea. They can be a little difficult at times."

"Well, give the vacuum a try," Harvey said.

Sabrina made sure that Salem was firmly in the pink basket before stepping onto the base of the vacuum cleaner. Immediately she noticed a difference—she had never stood on a vacuum without magic before. This time she nearly slipped off as soon as she got on. Sabrina assumed that these types of vacuums were probably created for magic users who could use their powers to keep them safely onboard. She was going to have to hold on tightly if she wanted to arrive in Hoboken in one piece.

"Just grip the handle tightly when you want to take off," Harvey said.

"Hold on, Salem," she said, giving the cat a pat on the head. "Here we—"

"Oh, it's you," Richard Locksley said as he stepped out the back door of the coffeehouse. "I thought I heard voices out here. I was hoping it was your aunt."

"Nope," Sabrina replied, glad for the fact that Hilda and Zelda weren't around. "Haven't seen her for a while now."

"Aren't you supposed to be in the hospital?" he asked.

Sabrina was glad to know he wasn't part of the search party. However she was beginning to share in Zelda's concern over the fact that he kept showing up at the most inopportune times asking questions of a suspicious nature.

"Oh, you know how those doctors work their magic," she said, using an intentional pun, hoping to throw him off. "I'm fine now."

"Even so," he replied. "Do you think you should be flying so soon after leaving the hospital?"

"No problem," she replied. "Do it all the time. You can go back inside and wait for Aunt Hilda. No need to worry."

"Just the same," he said, "I think I should at least stay here for takeoff. In case you have any lingering illness that could impair your flying."

"I'll be fine," Sabrina said, hoping to get rid of him. "And if anything goes wrong, I've got Harvey here."

Harvey gave the man a halfhearted little smile and wave, having no idea what exactly was going on.

"I think you aunt would prefer that I stuck around," Richard said. "To make sure you're not hurt."

Yeah, I bet that's why you're interested, she thought.

Stepping back onto the vacuum, Sabrina grasped tightly onto the handle. She could feel the motor whirring beneath her feet. Usually she just used her magic to make her vacuum go, but now she was going to have to immediately learn how to work the handle. Pulling back on it like a joystick, she felt the vacuum rise off the ground, which elicited a smile from her. "See you later," she said, bravely taking one hand off the handle to wave to Richard so that he could see how well she handled the machine.

"Bye, Sabrina," he replied. "If you see your aunt, please let her know I'm looking for her."

"Will do," Sabrina said as she watched him head back into the coffeehouse not a moment too soon. Once the door clicked closed, the vacuum dropped back down two feet, hitting the ground.

"Are you okay?" Harvey asked.

"No," Salem replied, even though the question was directed to Sabrina. When the vacuum hit the ground, however, Salem did a small flip in the basket and landed on his back.

"Sorry," Sabrina replied.

"You should keep both hands on the machine,"

Harvey said just a bit too late to do any good.

"At least Richard didn't see it," Sabrina replied, grabbing tightly onto the handle. "Here we go again."

"Whoopee," Salem said sarcastically.

"Have a safe flight," Harvey said as he watched Sabrina rise into the air as smoothly as she had the first time.

"Bye," Sabrina said as she lifted higher into the sky.

Once she cleared the top of the coffeehouse, Sabrina surveyed the area to make sure her aunts weren't around. It was hard to make people out from her height, but she was pretty sure the coast was clear. Looking down at the controls, she saw a compass and turned in a southward direction. "Hold on," Sabrina said as she leaned forward on the handle and slowly moved in that direction.

Coming out from between the buildings, Sabrina climbed a little higher into the air so that she was harder to spot from the ground. Feeling more comfortable, she leaned harder on the handle and wound up taking a deep dive. As the ground got closer, Sabrina pulled back quickly and launched herself up back into the air.

"I think I'm going to lose my lunch," Salem said from the basket. "Can't you keep this thing straight?"

"Would you like to fly it?" Sabrina asked as they zoomed through the air rather erratically.

"Tree!" he yelled as Sabrina swung the handle to the left just in the nick of time and managed to avoid becoming part of the foliage.

Once she passed the treetops, she could hear a siren behind her.

"That's never a good sound," Salem said. "Trust me, I know about these things."

Sabrina looked back over her shoulder and saw a traffic cop on a vacuum motioning her to pull over.

"What are you doing?" Salem asked as he could feel the vacuum slowing.

"Pulling over," Sabrina replied.

"Are you crazy?" he yelled. "If he figures out you're mortal and shouldn't be flying this thing, we'll never get to the Witches' Council."

"I can't just break the law," Sabrina replied.

"Is that all you're worried about?" Salem asked incredulously. "Have you noticed how the rules have kind of changed lately? And they're never going to change back unless we get to Hoboken."

Without waiting for a reply, Salem jumped from the basket onto the handle, pulling it down toward him. The vacuum lurched forward as their speed increased, as well as their proximity to the ground. Sabrina slapped Salem away from the handle and pulled back on it as the cat fell into the basket. Narrowly avoiding the ground, Sabrina realized that they were now officially in a police chase.

Refusing to look back, Sabrina continued flying as fast as the vacuum could take her, holding on for dear life. Winding left and right through the trees, she could hear the siren of the police vacuum following her. She tried to figure out a good story to explain her erratic flying to the cop, but finally realized that Salem was right. It was more important to fix the world than to worry about getting pulled over for bad flying.

"I can't fly all the way to Hoboken with the police on my tail," Sabrina said to Salem.

"We need to go someplace to lose them," Salem said. "How about to your campus? You know that area pretty well."

"But my aunts could be back there looking for me," Sabrina replied. "I don't need them joining the chase."

Sabrina dove to miss a flock of birds traveling in her path. From the sounds behind her, she guessed that the police officer didn't quite manage to avoid the entire flock. "The Freedom Trail!" she exclaimed.

"What about it?" Salem asked.

"I spent all yesterday afternoon on it," Sabrina

replied. "I think I know where we can lose him."

"To the Freedom Trail!" Salem yelled. "How appropriate."

Sabrina banked left as she swung the vacuum in the direction of Boston Common. She figured once around the park could be enough to get the cop off their tail. Seeing the public park up ahead, Sabrina dove into the trees, trying to hide. She could still hear the siren closing in on her. Then she heard another siren joining in.

Daring to look back as she weaved in and out of the trees, Sabrina saw they had been joined by another traffic cop on a vacuum. Now she had to lose both of them.

"Another tree!" Salem yelled again as Sabrina faced forward and flung them to the right and past the obstacle.

Looking down, Sabrina realized she was above the grove where the statue of Richard used to be. Then she was flying next to the park fountain, which was now magically shooting two hundred feet into the air and changing colors. She could see a little boy laughing as he pointed to the giant waterspout.

"To the trail!" Salem yelled. He was really getting into the excitement of the chase.

Sabrina headed for the new State house as she looked down and saw Christy Caldwell interviewing some mortal girls by the frog pond. She could have almost sworn that the girls were turning the frogs into handsome princes, but she was moving so fast on the vacuum that she couldn't be exactly sure of what she was seeing.

Continuing toward the State house, Sabrina glanced back to see the two vacuums were still following and even gaining on her. As she reached the State house, she circled the dome while planning her next move. Luckily the police kept the same distance from her as they circled as well. Sabrina just hoped that neither of them would decide to stop suddenly, or else she would crash into them. And that would end the chase quickly.

"I'm getting dizzy," Salem complained as they circled the dome for the fifth time.

"Stop being a front-basket driver," Sabrina hollered as she suddenly dove away from the dome, hoping to surprise her followers.

The plan seemed to work as the cops took one additional loop around the dome before getting back on her tail. Continuing her dive, Sabrina weaved in and out of the State house statuary and could hear one of the vacuums crash behind her. Sabrina glanced back to make sure the policeman was okay. Seeing that he had pointed up a fluffy pile of pillows to fall on and was fine, she continued on with only one cop trailing her.

Passing the Park Street Church and King's Chapel, Sabrina continued onto the site of the first public school. The reporter in her couldn't help but think up even more story ideas that she hoped to pitch to Christy if she and Salem ever managed to evade the police, get to Hoboken, and fix the world.

Coming up on the statue of Benjamin Franklin, Sabrina noticed that the cop was almost right on top of her. Thinking quickly, she had a brainstorm that she hoped would get them out of this mess. "Salem, I've got an idea," Sabrina said excitedly. "Give me a claw."

"They're not removable," he replied.

Grabbing Salem by the arm, Sabrina pulled him out of the basket.

"Watch it!" he yelled. "I'm delicate."

Sabrina chose to ignore that last comment as she made sure his claws were out. Taking his left paw, she ran it down the side of the vacuum bag, ripping it in two. Within moments, dirt and dust were billowing out behind them and right at their follower.

Sabrina watched as the traffic cop got lost in the cloud of dust and his vacuum dropped out of the air, landing softly in a patch of bushes.

"Eat our dust, copper!" Salem yelled to the ground.

"Salem, I think you're enjoying this a little too much," Sabrina said.

"Can we do it again?" he asked excitedly.

Chapter 13

It didn't take long for Sabrina and Salem to fly to Hoboken, although they did run into a few minor magical problems along the way. The largest obstacle they had to overcome was that at one point the clouds became so thick, Sabrina had to maneuver around them instead of just fly through them. Eventually they made their way to the destination. The only problem was they didn't know where to go once they got there.

"Now I know the one very important question we forgot to ask," Salem said as Sabrina took the vacuum cleaner in for a landing.

"Hoboken's a lot bigger than I had imagined," Sabrina agreed. "How are we ever going to find the Witches' Council, especially if they meet in secret?"

"Somehow that seems too logical for the Witches' Council," Salem said as he hopped out of the basket and padded his way over to a nearby phone booth.

"What are you doing?" Sabrina asked as she followed him.

"Playing a hunch," he replied as he hopped up to the phone book that was on a shelf. Sliding his paws over the book, her turned the pages until he found what he was looking for. "Aha!"

"Aha, what?" Sabrina asked, looking over his shoulder.

"Look under legal organizations," he replied proudly as he pushed the phone book toward her.

Sabrina picked up the book and skimmed the page he had turned to, but she couldn't find a thing. Then Salem pointed his paw to an ad in the lower right-hand corner of the page, smiling at her.

"'World Incorporated Transatlantic Commission of Hoboken Council,'" Sabrina read. "That makes absolutely no sense whatsoever."

"Look closer," he said.

Sabrina did as he said, and this time she noticed something about the strange collection of words. "Witches' Council!" she yelled as she realized that the first letter of each of the words in the company name spelled out what she was looking for.

"Leave it to the Council to advertise a secret

organization," Salem said. "I guess they're the same in any reality."

"I don't have any paper to write the address on," Sabrina said.

"Just rip out the page," Salem suggested.

"First evading the police, now vandalism," Sabrina said. "What kind of trouble are you getting me into?"

"When the world goes back to normal, I'm sure the page will repair itself," Salem said as he tore it out with his paws. "Come on."

Sabrina and Salem hopped back onto the vacuum and headed for the address listed on the page. Their excitement level was growing as they neared their goal. After a few twists and turns down the different streets of Hoboken, they came across an old building that looked somewhat reminiscent of a courthouse. The only problem, Sabrina realized as they circled the place, was that there were no doors.

"This must be the place," Sabrina said, taking the vacuum down for a landing. "But how do we get in?"

"Why can't anything ever be easy?" Salem asked, not expecting an answer.

"Maybe they're using a Mortals-Keep-Out spell," Sabrina suggested. "Like the one back in that crazy store I was in."

"Okay," he said. "So how do we find the door?"

"Well, I flung myself against the wall the first time," Sabrina said, remembering back to the alley in Boston.

"There's a lot of wall here to fling ourselves against," Salem said looking around. "There has to be an easier way. Possibly one that doesn't have the same potential for pain."

"Maybe we should just scream until someone lets us in," Sabrina meekly suggested.

"Not exactly the most stealthy way to make an entrance," Salem replied. "This is ridiculous. You think they'd design the building so witches could get in easily."

"Let's see if there's a clue on the page you tore from the phone book," Sabrina said as she pulled the paper from her pocket and unfolded it.

"See, I knew it would come in handy," Salem said, still trying to justify his little act of vandalism.

Sabrina scanned the ad for the Witches' Council and read it aloud for Salem's benefit. "'World Incorporated Transatlantic Commission of Hoboken Council. A safe haven for those who feel powerless.'"

"Well that's certainly us," Salem said.

"What?" Sabrina asked, still studying the ad.

"Powerless."

As soon as the word was out of his mouth, a sign appeared in front of them.

Stepping up to the sign, Sabrina read it aloud. "'Just say a spell and come on in.'"

"If we could do that we wouldn't need to go in," Salem replied.

"Why did that sign appear?" Sabrina asked.

"Beats me," Salem said. "I didn't do anything."

"It appeared when you said 'powerless,'" Sabrina replied as yet another sign popped up on the wall. It said the same thing as the first sign: JUST SAY A SPELL AND COME ON IN.

"Well, we're starting a nice little collection," Salem said. "But unless we're going into business selling signs, I don't see how this is going to help."

"Obviously saying 'powerless' is a password," Sabrina said.

"And how does that help us with this spell they want us to say?" Salem asked.

"Let's think about this," Sabrina replied. "The Council wouldn't require a witch to cast a spell—witches can't cast spells here, remember?"

Sabrina thought over the phrase. *Just say a spell and come on in.* And then it dawned on Sabrina: At first she couldn't believe the answer was that simple—the Witches' Council was ridiculously literal no matter what reality they were in. She stepped up to the wall. "A spell!"

Suddenly she and Salem were transported inside the building.

"Well, that was a pointless—" Salem started to say.

Sabrina cut him off by pulling Salem into her arms as they followed signs to the Witches' Council Chambers. All the while Sabrina tried to figure out what she was going to say. It was certainly one thing to get to the Witches' Council; now she needed them to make everything right again.

Sabrina pushed open the door to the Witches' Council Chambers and saw a row of oddly dressed people sitting behind a long table. They appeared to be arguing over something, but Sabrina couldn't make out what they were talking about. "Excuse me," she said politely.

The Council ignored her as they continued their argument.

"Hello?" she asked, wondering if they even noticed her standing there.

"Hey!" Salem yelled.

The Council immediately froze as a look of horror passed over each member's face.

"What are you doing bringing a familiar in here!" the red-headed councilwoman at the end of the table demanded of Sabrina. "No mortal familiars are allowed in these chambers."

"He's not a mortal familiar," Sabrina said. "He's a witch familiar."

"There's no such thing as a witch familiar," the woman snidely remarked.

"That's why I'm here to see you," Sabrina said, still holding Salem in her arms.

"Sorry, we don't see anyone after business hours," another councilwoman said.

"But it's not five o'clock yet," Sabrina replied, trying not to stare at the other woman's incredibly overdone makeup job.

"It most certainly is," a man wearing a monocle said. "In numerous places in the world it is well after five o'clock."

"Oh, yeah, we're in the right place," Salem said.

"You can come back tomorrow," the red-haired woman said before turning back to the rest of the Council to continue their fight.

"No, we can't," Sabrina interjected before they could start up again. "This is very important."

"Well, if it's important, you'll most certainly have to come back tomorrow," the woman insisted. "Our presiding witch judge is out of town at the moment, and we cannot make any decisions without him."

"But there are six of you on the Council," Sabrina said. "Can't any of you help?"

"Certainly not," the woman said, as if it was the most logical response in the world.

"Where is Drell when you need him?" Salem asked rhetorically.

"Saskatchewan," a man at the other end of the table replied.

"Look," Sabrina said, addressing the Council, "I don't care if the judge isn't around right now. We've got a big problem, and I need your help to fix it."

"Why should we?" the woman with the makeup difficulties asked.

"Because you're the Witches' Council," Sabrina replied, frustrated that they were being even more difficult to deal with than they had been when they had magical powers.

"Did we cause this problem?" the redhead asked.

"Well . . . no," Sabrina reluctantly answered.

"Then I fail to see how it is our responsibility," the woman said.

Sabrina was about to give up.

"However . . . ," the redhead continued.

Immediately Sabrina perked right up.

"Since you did come all the way from Boston," the woman continued.

"How did you know we're from Boston?" Sabrina asked.

"We *are* the Witches' Council," the man at the

other end of the table said, causing the entire Council to giggle as if he had made a joke.

"I do not like these people," Salem whispered to Sabrina through clenched teeth.

"Please tell us the problem," the man with the monocle said. "But make it quick. It's nearing midnight in certain parts of the world."

Sabrina had no idea what that piece of information had to do with their current situation, but she ignored the man and began her story. She explained everything, starting with the reason why she had cast the See-Things-Through-My-Eyes spell. Then she explained how she had changed the spell, and all the crazy things that had resulted. By the time she was finished cataloging the chain of events, she wasn't sure if the Council was paying rapt attention to her or if they had all slipped into comas.

"And that's when I realized I shouldn't try to prove to my friends how hard my life is, since everyone has a rough life from time to time," Sabrina said, concluding her tale.

"What a wonderful story," said an elderly man dressed entirely in blue from head to toe. "Now what do you want us to do about it?"

"Don't you get it?" she asked. "I learned my lesson. You can turn everything back to normal."

"Obviously you weren't listening to us," the red-headed woman said. "We can't do anything without the presiding witch judge present."

"And here I am," Dr. Young said as he came into the chamber with Sabrina's aunts following closely behind him.

The doctor took a seat in the center of the council table before a very shocked Sabrina and Salem could say a word.

"What are you doing here?" Sabrina asked her aunts and her former therapist.

"I'm the current presiding judge," Dr. Young replied.

"We had looked for you everywhere else," Zelda said. "So we assumed you must have come here."

"How did you get here, by the way?" Hilda asked.

"Harvey's vacuum," Sabrina replied. "But can someone explain what it going on?"

"We're here to counteract your spell," Dr. Young said, although Sabrina was beginning to suspect that he wasn't a real doctor.

"Why don't we take this again from the top?" Sabrina asked.

"It was the See-Things-Through-My-Eyes spell that you cast," Zelda explained.

"So now you believe I cast a spell," Sabrina said. "But how did you know what it was called?"

"It's a trick spell," Hilda said. "As soon as a witch casts it, the Council is immediately notified.

Then they called us for our help in casting the alternate reality spell. Everything you've been through today has been because of us. Surprise!"

Sabrina shot Salem a dirty look.

"How was I supposed to know?" he said indignantly. "It wasn't in the fine print."

"So changing the words of the spell had nothing to do with it?" Sabrina asked.

"Nope," Hilda replied.

"You see, Sabrina," Zelda explained. "The Council realized long ago that when a witch casts a See-Things-Through-My-Eyes spell, she is the one who really needs to see the world differently. It was only once you stopped worrying about impressing your friends that you could truly understand that it doesn't matter whether they know how hard your life is. The main thing is that *you* see your accomplishments for what they are and not by how others perceive them."

"Yeah, I figured that out way back at the hospital with you," Sabrina said as she pointed to the witch judge formerly known as Dr. Young. "Why didn't the spell end back then?"

"Well, we came in to tell you everything after you spoke with Judge Young," Zelda said. "But you had gone out the window."

"I have to say, you did a great job getting away from us," Hilda said. "Even managed to elude the mortal police we sent after you."

"But why didn't you just end the spell?" Sabrina asked the judge. "Everything would have gone back to normal, and I would have stopped running."

"One of the rules of the spell is that it can't be reversed until the witch is told the truth," Judge Young replied. "If we couldn't find you, we couldn't reverse the spell."

"You know, you guys should maybe think about rewriting some of these rules so that they don't cause so much trouble for witches," Sabrina said.

"If we did that," the red-headed woman said, "we'd all be out of jobs."

Sabrina couldn't argue with that little piece of logic.

"So can we all go back to be being normal witches now?" Sabrina asked.

"I knew it!" Richard Locksley yelled as he stepped into the Witches' Council Chambers. "Hilda, you're a witch. I was right all along, and now I'm going to expose you to the world."

"Oh, for crying out loud," Hilda said as she pointed her finger and turned her boyfriend back to stone.

There was a momentary silence in the room.

"So how does Richard Locksley fit into all this?" Sabrina asked.

"He was just a little bonus," Hilda said. "I took

this opportunity to get Zelda to agree to temporarily turn him back. I wanted to prove finally whether he was trying to expose me as a witch."

"If it had turned out that he wasn't," Zelda continued, "then I was going to help convince Mother to turn him back permanently."

"I guess that won't be happening now," Hilda said.

"I'm so sorry," Zelda said to her sister, and she truly meant it.

"Well, it's best to know once and for all," Hilda replied as she magically sent the statue of Richard back to his spot in the park.

"But what about my friends and the rest of the world?" Sabrina asked.

"Nothing really happened to them," the judge explained. "This was all created for your benefit. When you wake up tomorrow, it will be today again."

"Wonderful," Sabrina said sarcastically. "You all certainly went to a whole lot of trouble just to prove a lesson to me."

"It beats doing the daily paperwork," Judge Young said.

"But why was I put through all this too?" Salem demanded.

"You suggested the spell in the first place," Zelda said.

Hilda and Zelda said their thanks to the

Witches' Council, but Sabrina had some trouble expressing gratitude for being put through the wringer. They did, however, manage to zap themselves home before Salem had a chance to express his anger toward the Witches' Council for being included in Sabrina's lesson of the day.

Back at home the Spellmans collapsed on the couch, exhausted.

"Since the world isn't going back to normal until you go to sleep," Zelda said to her niece, "why don't you stay here tonight? We can whip up a nice family dinner."

"That sounds great," Sabrina said. "Besides I'm too tired to move. Do you want to do the magical cooking, Aunt Hilda? I hear you're a great cook."

"Actually, I have an errand to run first," Hilda replied.

"Oh, really?" Zelda said. "Where are you going?"

"Just a little trip to the park," Hilda said.

"But I thought you were over Richard," Sabrina said.

"Oh, I am," Hilda replied, and she magically zapped up a two-pound bag of birdseed. "I just thought it was time for a new tradition. I know a few dozen pigeons who could use a new place to nest."

About the Author

Paul Ruditis is also the author of *Sabrina, the Teenage Witch #37: Witch Way Did She Go?* He has also written and contributed to several books based on such notable television series as *Buffy, the Vampire Slayer*, *Roswell*, *Enterprise*, and *The West Wing*.

Gaze into the future and see what wonders lie in store
for Sabrina, the Teenage Witch

#45 Hounded by Baskervilles

When Sabrina doesn't have the time to finish reading
the classic novel The Hound of the Baskervilles,
she summons the main character and famous sleuth,
Sherlock Holmes, to give her the 411 on the book.
But when Sabrina's professor brings his dog
Baskerville to class, Sabrina has a magical allergic
reaction that nearly turns the Mortal Realm into the
Animal Kingdom.